# ARF AND the METAL DETECTOR
## by Philip Wooderson

ILLUSTRATED BY BRIDGET MACKEITH

**Librarian Reviewer**
Allyson A.W. Lyga
Library Media/Graphic Novel Consultant
Fulbright Memorial Fund Scholar, author

**Reading Consultant**
Elizabeth Stedem
Educator/Consultant, Colorado Springs, CO
M.A. in Elementary Education, University of Denver, CO

 **STONE ARCH BOOKS**
Minneapolis  San Diego

First published in the United States in 2007
by Stone Arch Books,
151 Good Counsel Drive, P.O. Box 669,
Mankato, Minnesota 56002.
www.stonearchbooks.com

Originally published in Great Britain in 2001
by A & C Black Publishers Ltd,
38 Soho Square, London, W1D 3HB.

Library of Congress Cataloging-in-Publication Data
Wooderson, Philip.
    Arf and the Metal Detector / by Philip Wooderson; illustrated by Bridget Mackeith.
    p. cm. — (Graphic Trax)
    ISBN-13: 978-1-59889-085-3 (hardcover)
    ISBN-10: 1-59889-085-9 (hardcover)
    ISBN-13: 978-1-59889-231-4 (paperback)
    ISBN-10: 1-59889-231-2 (paperback)
    1. Graphic novels. I. MacKeith, Bridget. II. Title. III. Series.
PN6727.W66A75 2007
741.5'973—dc22                                          2006006068

Summary: Arf can't help himself. When a package for his neighbor shows up at his house, Arf has to see what's inside. The package leads him to more trouble, a couple of crooks, and a buried treasure.

Art Director: Heather Kindseth
Colorist: Steve Christensen
Graphic Designer: Kay Fraser
Production Artist: Keegan Gilbert

1 2 3 4 5 6 11 10 09 08 07 06

Printed in the United States of America

# TABLE OF CONTENTS

N

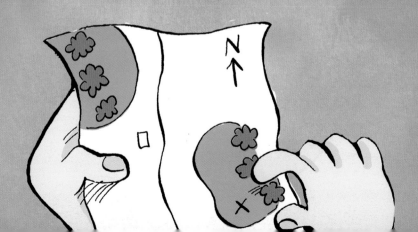

# CAST OF CHARACTERS

ARF

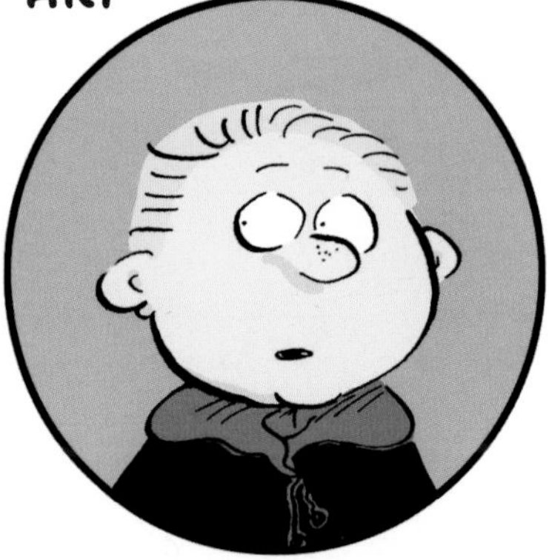

GLORIA

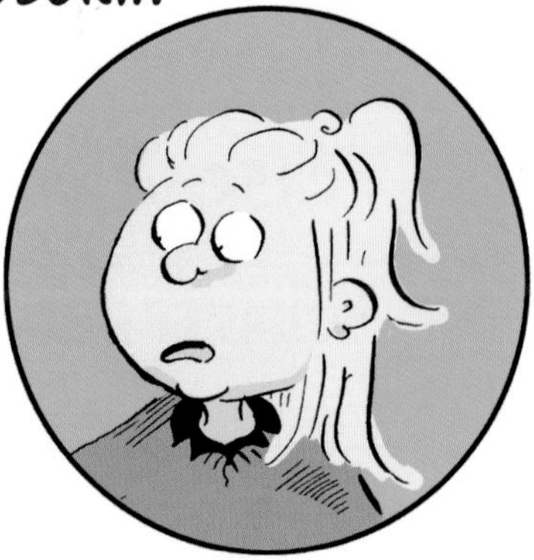

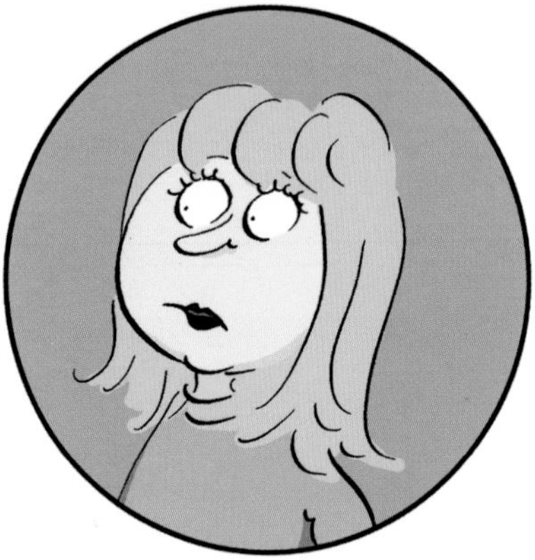

MOM

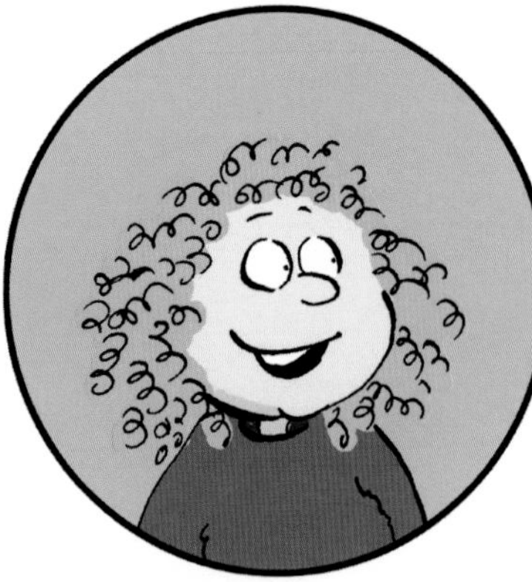

BEE

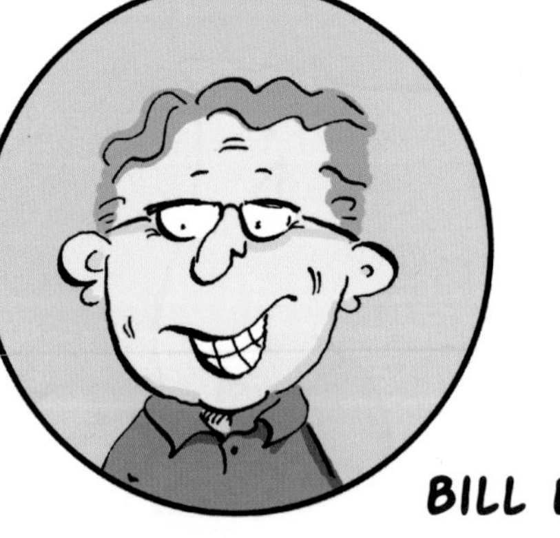

BILL BOTT

# CHAPTER ONE

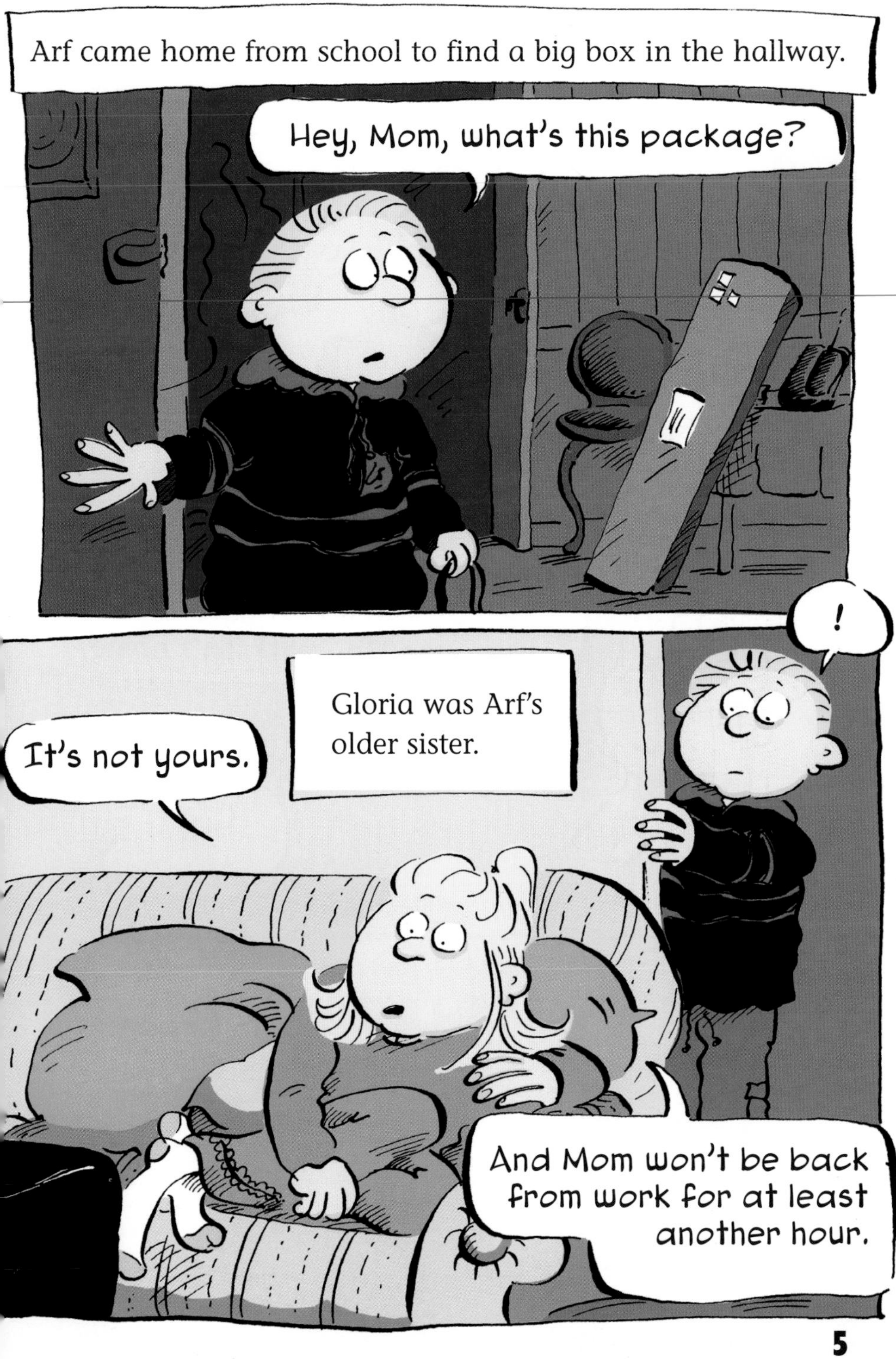
Arf came home from school to find a big box in the hallway.
Hey, Mom, what's this package?
!
It's not yours.
Gloria was Arf's older sister.
And Mom won't be back from work for at least another hour.

Arf looked at the address.

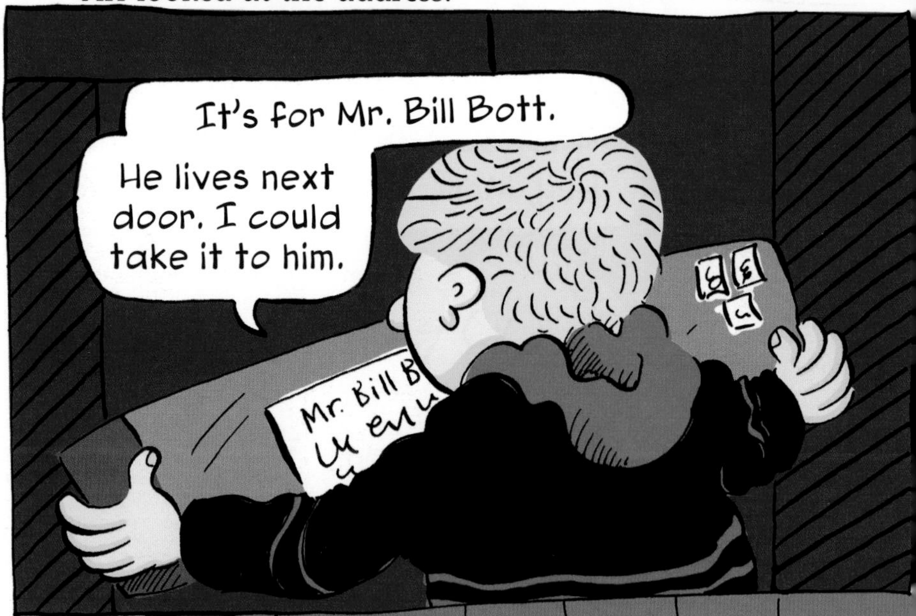
It's for Mr. Bill Bott.
He lives next door. I could take it to him.
Mr. Bill B

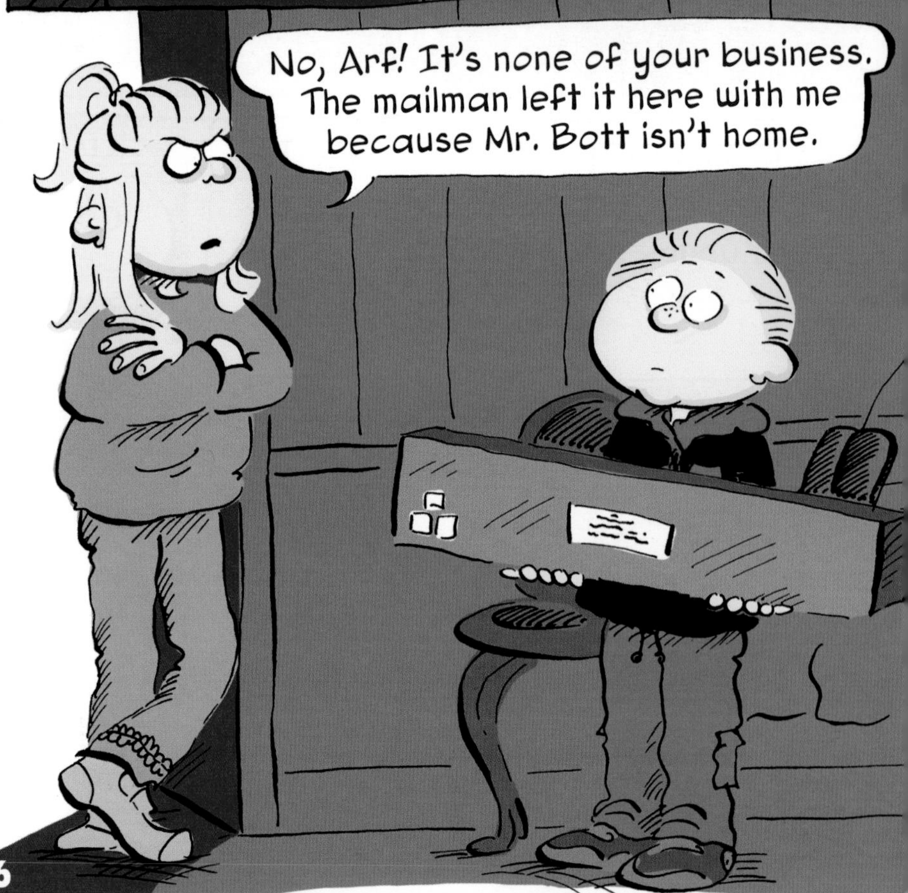
No, Arf! It's none of your business. The mailman left it here with me because Mr. Bott isn't home.

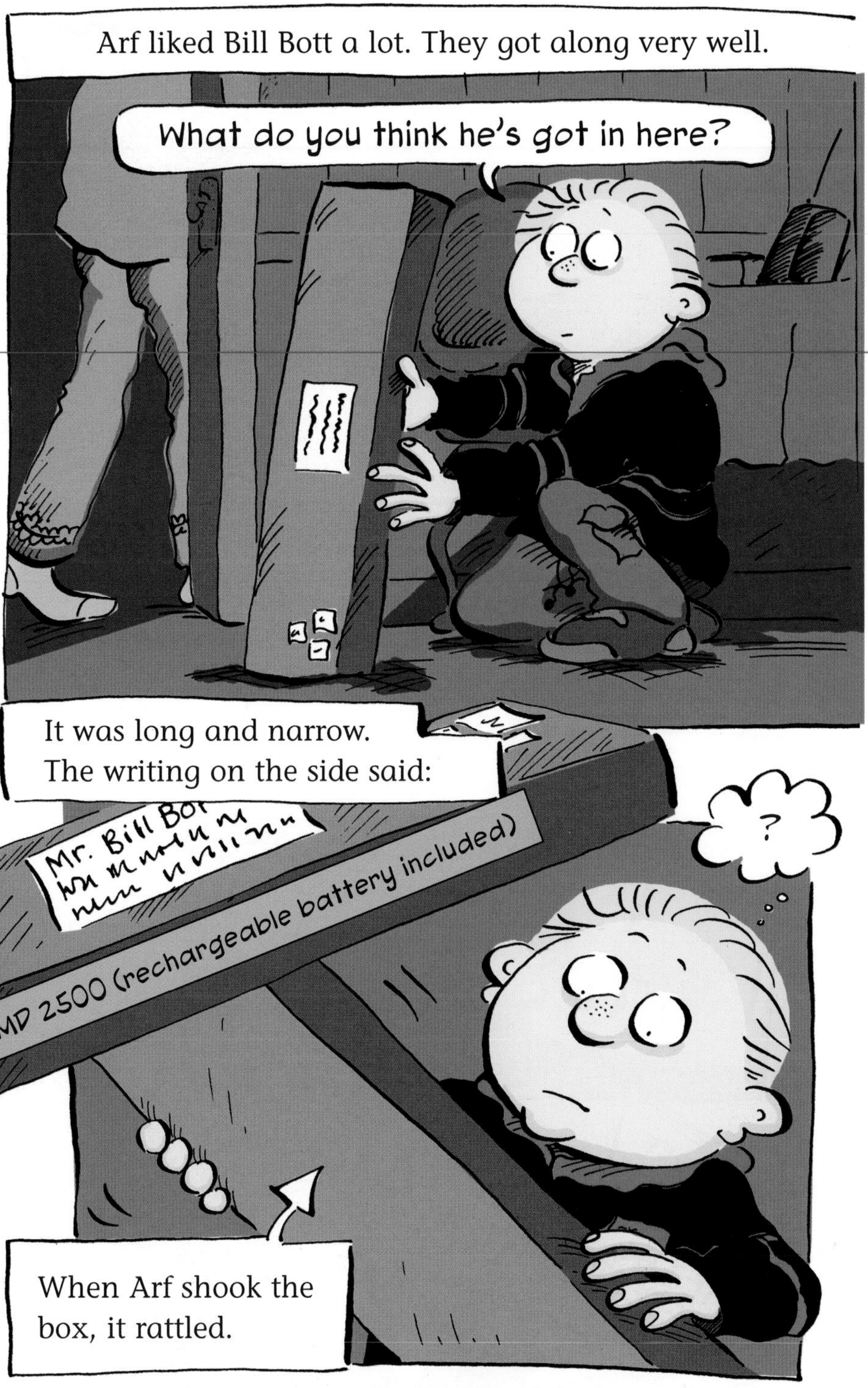
Arf liked Bill Bott a lot. They got along very well.
What do you think he's got in here?
It was long and narrow.
The writing on the side said:
MD 2500 (rechargeable battery included)
?
When Arf shook the box, it rattled.

The cardboard flap on the top end was sealed by a short piece of tape, until Arf peeled it off. Then he took a quick look inside.

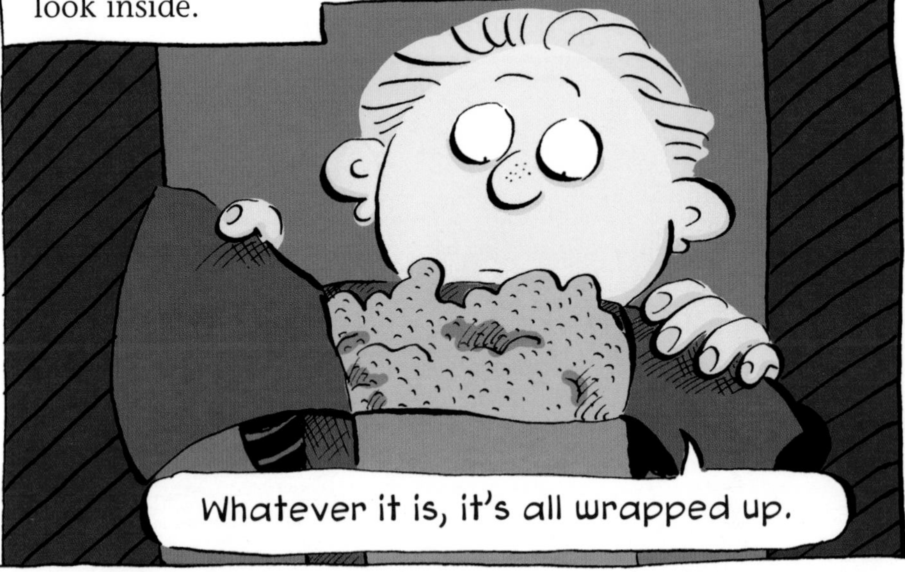
Whatever it is, it's all wrapped up.

Arf pushed his hand inside and pulled out a little booklet. He opened it to the first page.

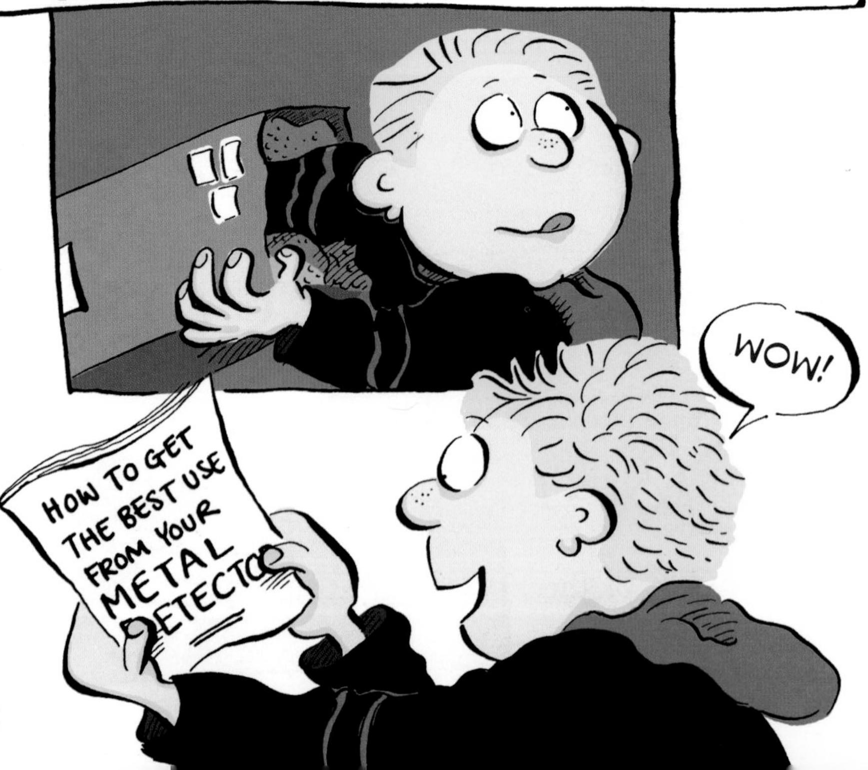
WOW!
HOW TO GET
THE BEST USE
FROM YOUR
METAL

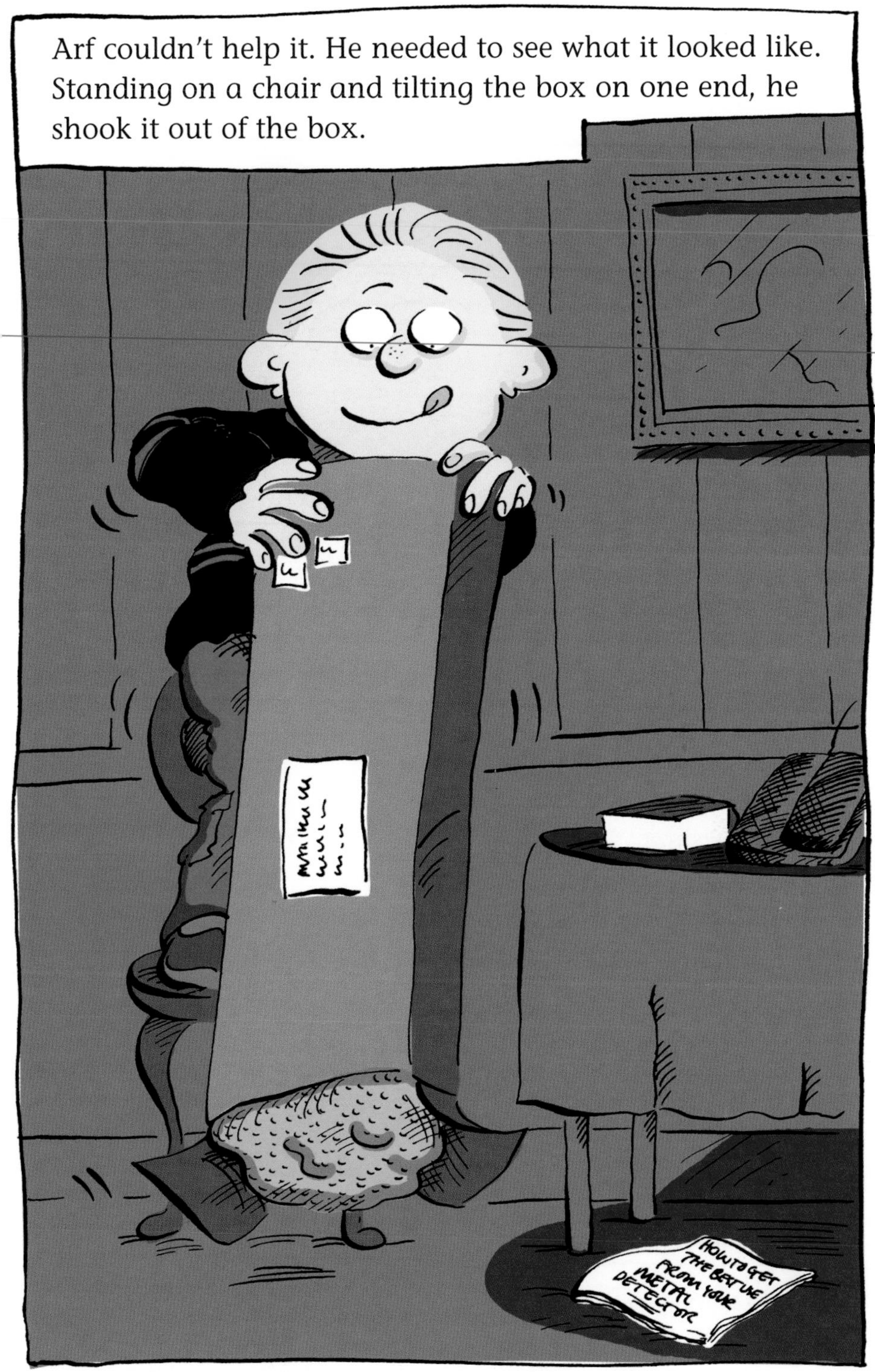
Arf couldn't help it. He needed to see what it looked like. Standing on a chair and tilting the box on one end, he shook it out of the box.
HOW TO GET THE BEST USE FROM YOUR METAL DETECTOR

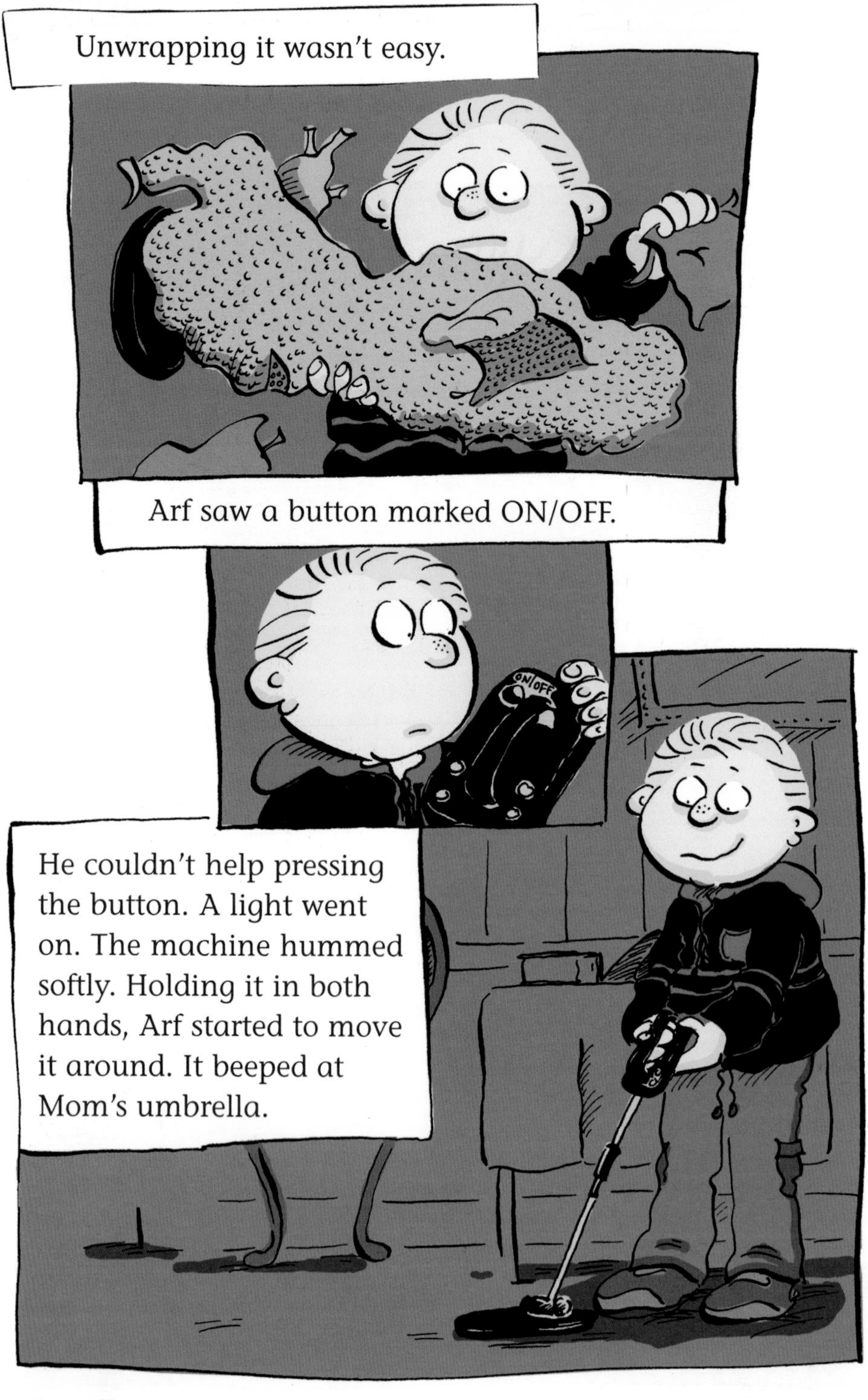
Unwrapping it wasn't easy.
Arf saw a button marked ON/OFF.
ON/OFF
He couldn't help pressing the button. A light went on. The machine hummed softly. Holding it in both hands, Arf started to move it around. It beeped at Mom's umbrella.

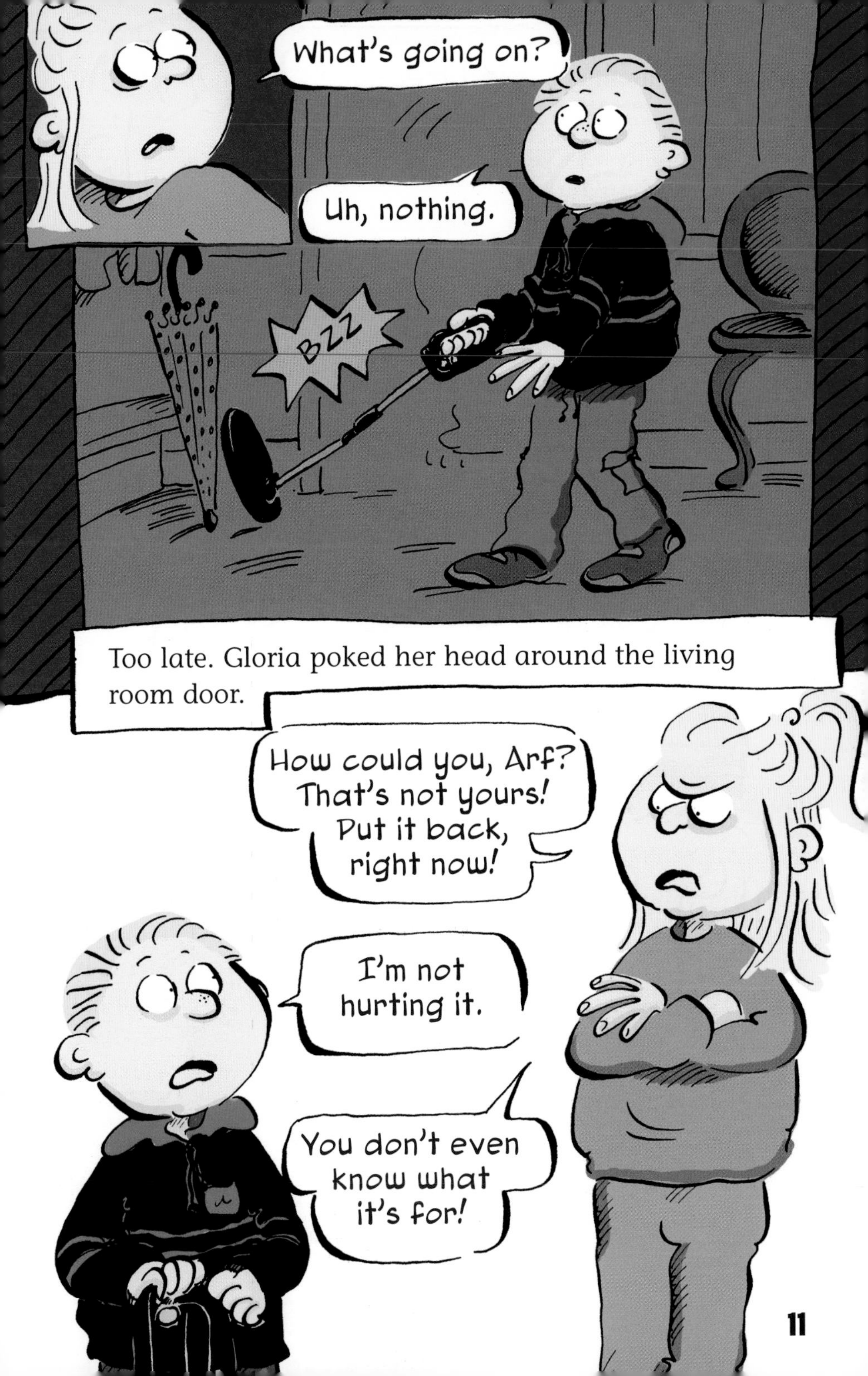
What's going on?
Uh, nothing.
BZZ
Too late. Gloria poked her head around the living room door.
How could you, Arf? That's not yours! Put it back, right now!
I'm not hurting it.
You don't even know what it's for!

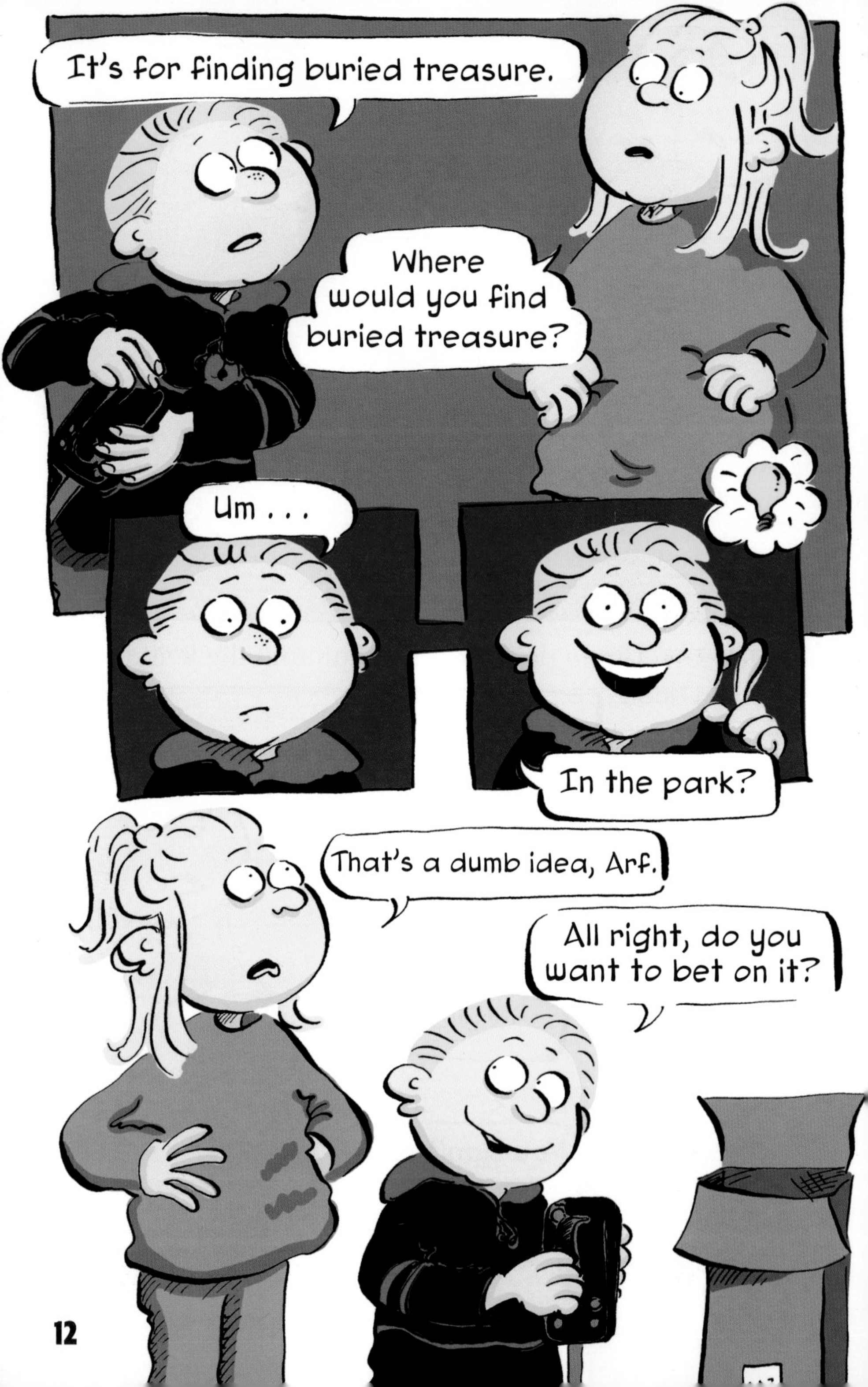
It's for finding buried treasure.
Where would you find buried treasure?
Um . . .
In the park?
That's a dumb idea, Arf.
All right, do you want to bet on it?

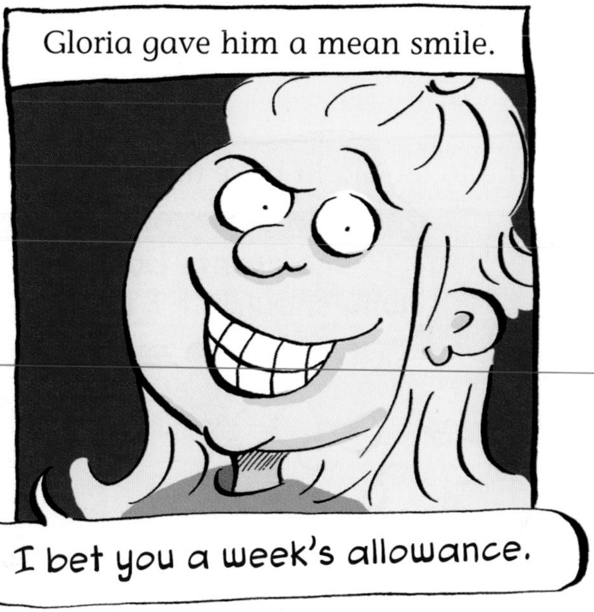
Gloria gave him a mean smile.
I bet you a week's allowance.

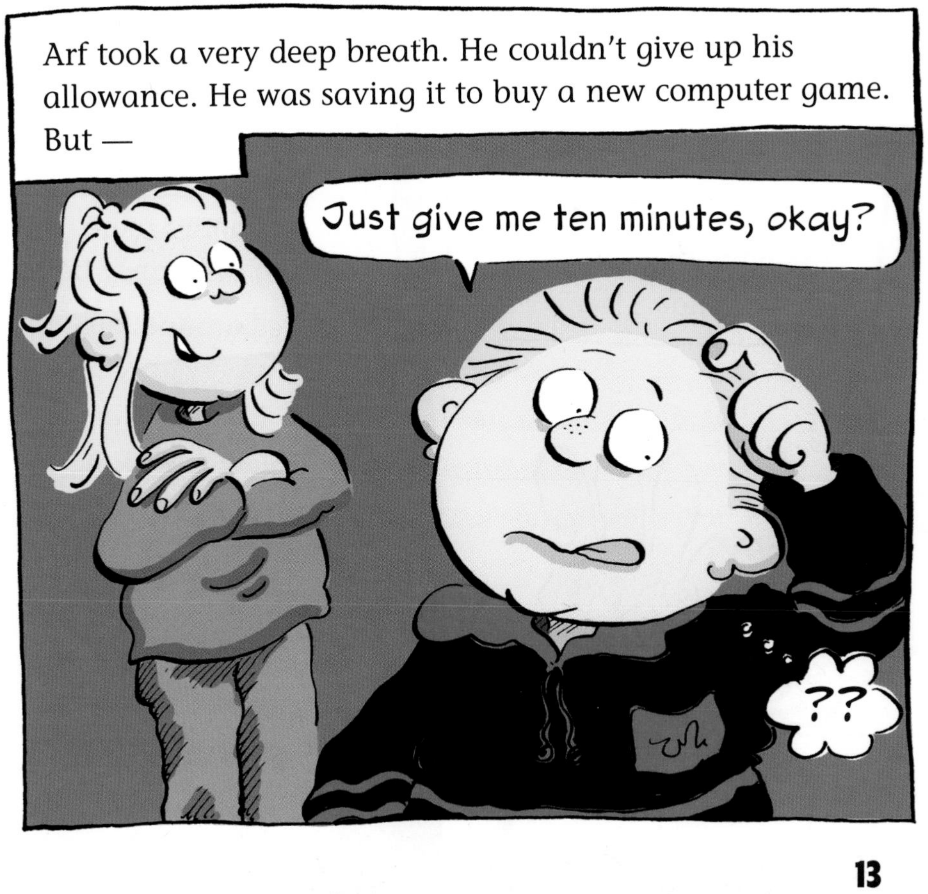
Arf took a very deep breath. He couldn't give up his allowance. He was saving it to buy a new computer game. But —
Just give me ten minutes, okay?
??

# CHAPTER TWO

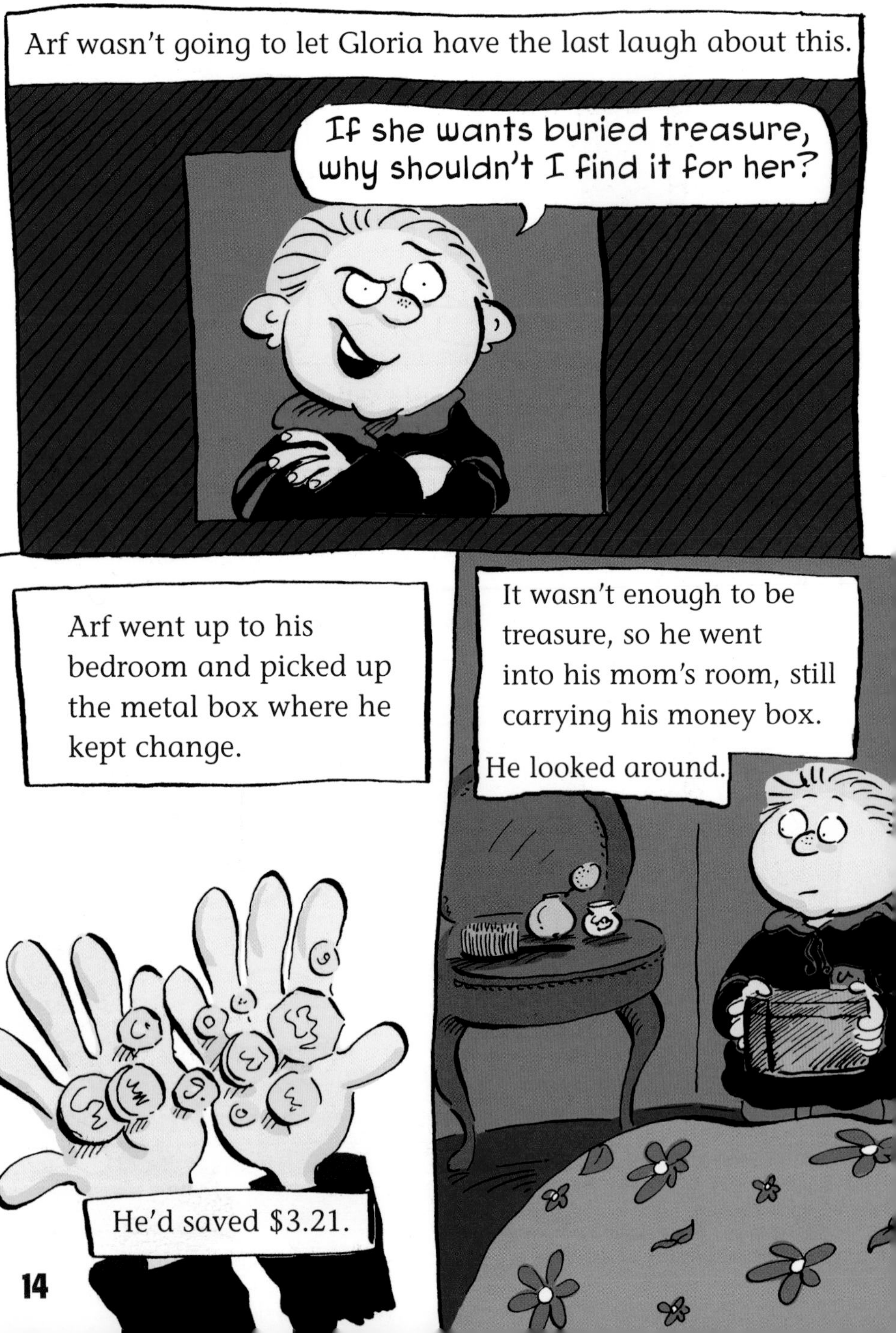
Arf wasn't going to let Gloria have the last laugh about this.
If she wants buried treasure, why shouldn't I find it for her?
Arf went up to his bedroom and picked up the metal box where he kept change.
He'd saved $3.21.
It wasn't enough to be treasure, so he went into his mom's room, still carrying his money box.
He looked around.

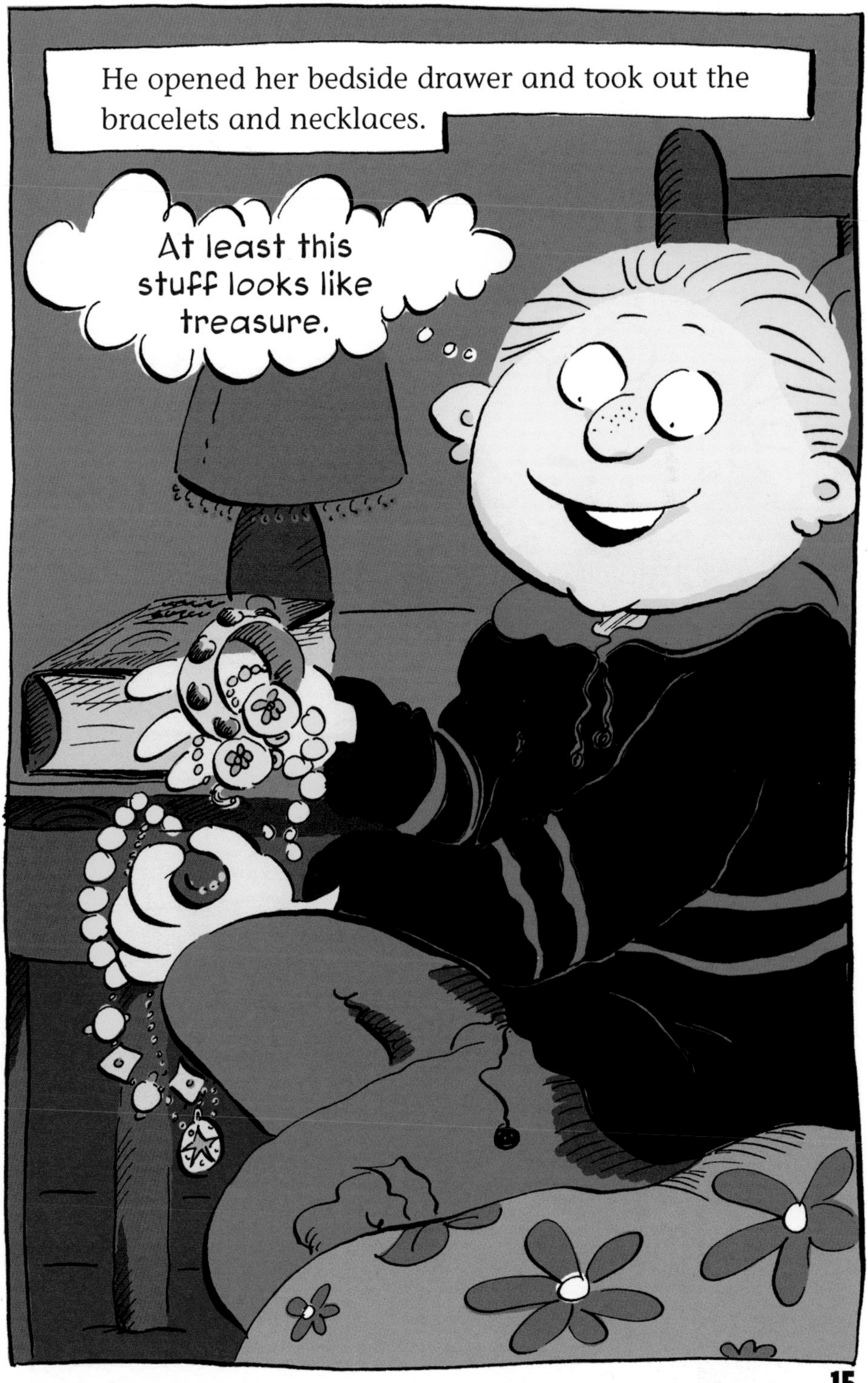
He opened her bedside drawer and took out the bracelets and necklaces.
At least this stuff looks like treasure.

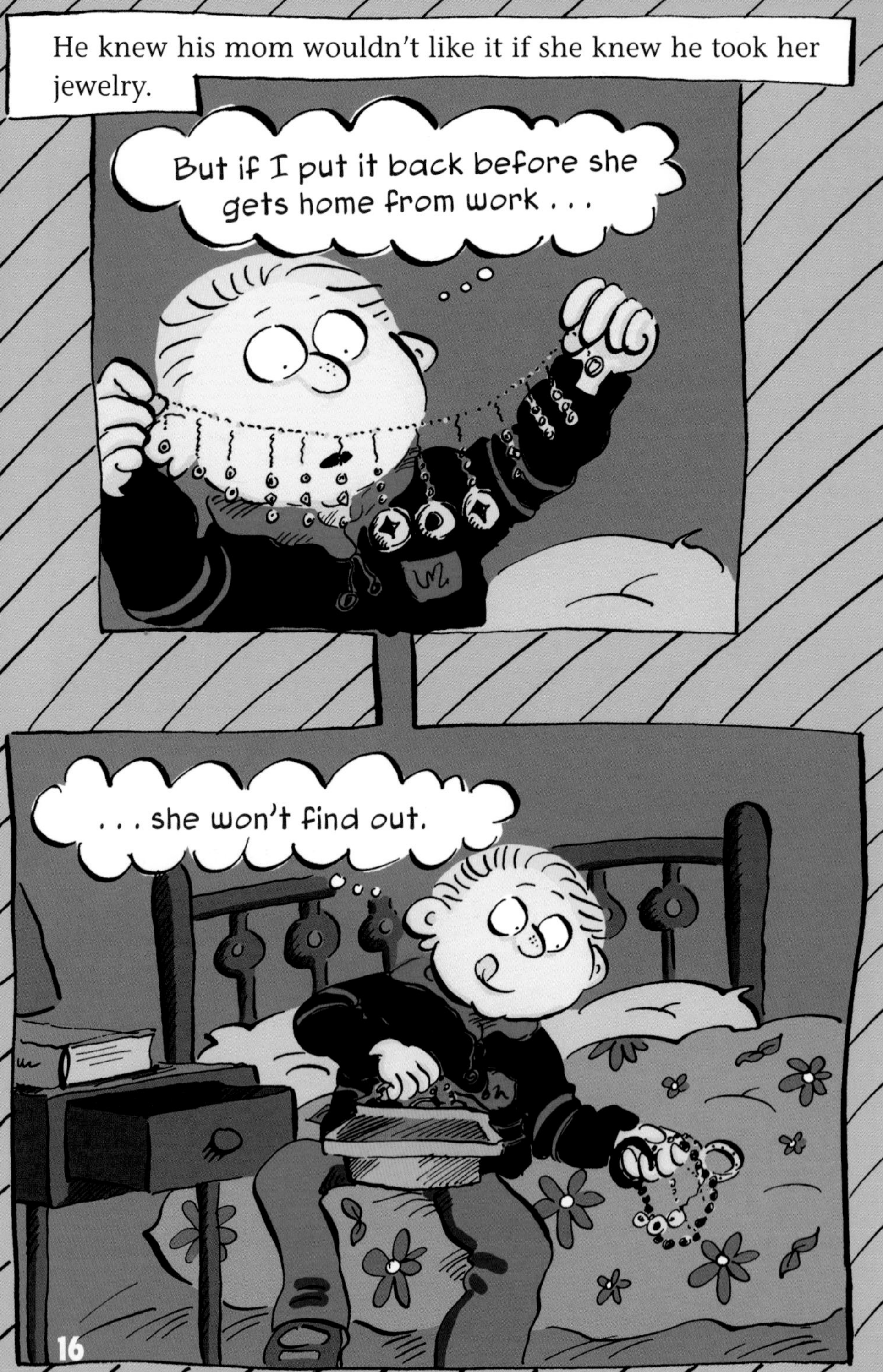
He knew his mom wouldn't like it if she knew he took her jewelry.
But if I put it back before she gets home from work . . .
. . . she won't find out.

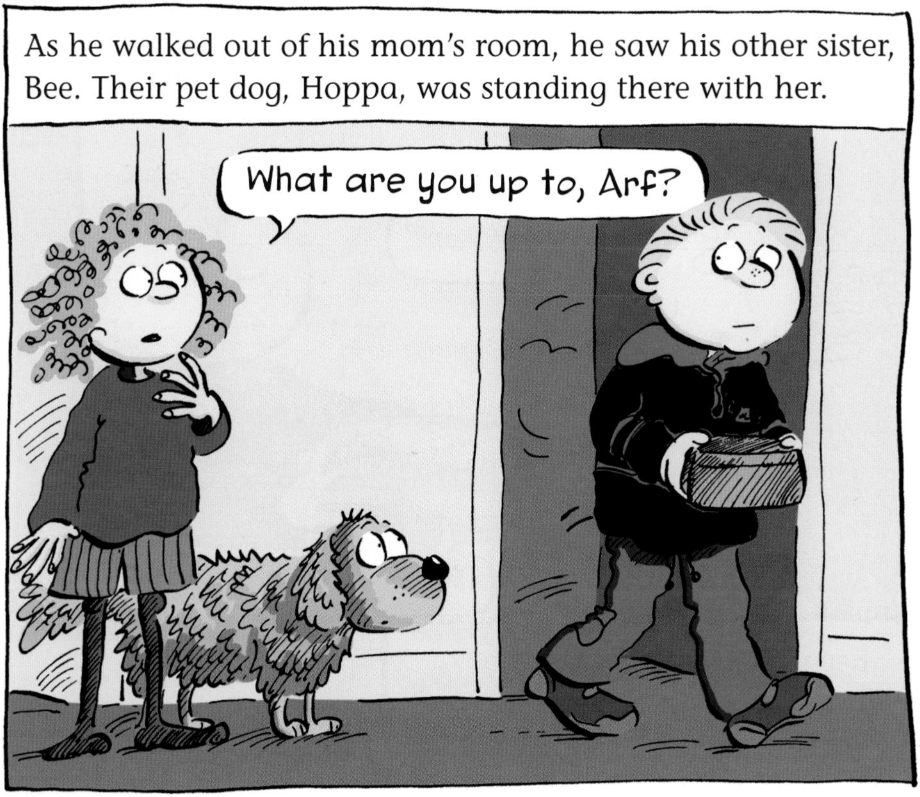
As he walked out of his mom's room, he saw his other sister, Bee. Their pet dog, Hoppa, was standing there with her.
What are you up to, Arf?

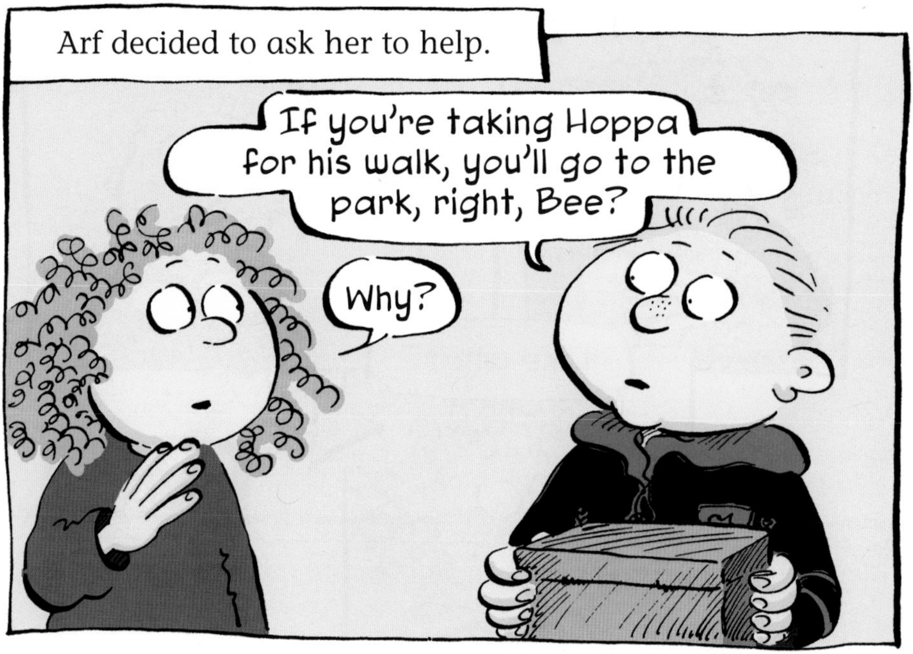
Arf decided to ask her to help.
If you're taking Hoppa for his walk, you'll go to the park, right, Bee?
Why?

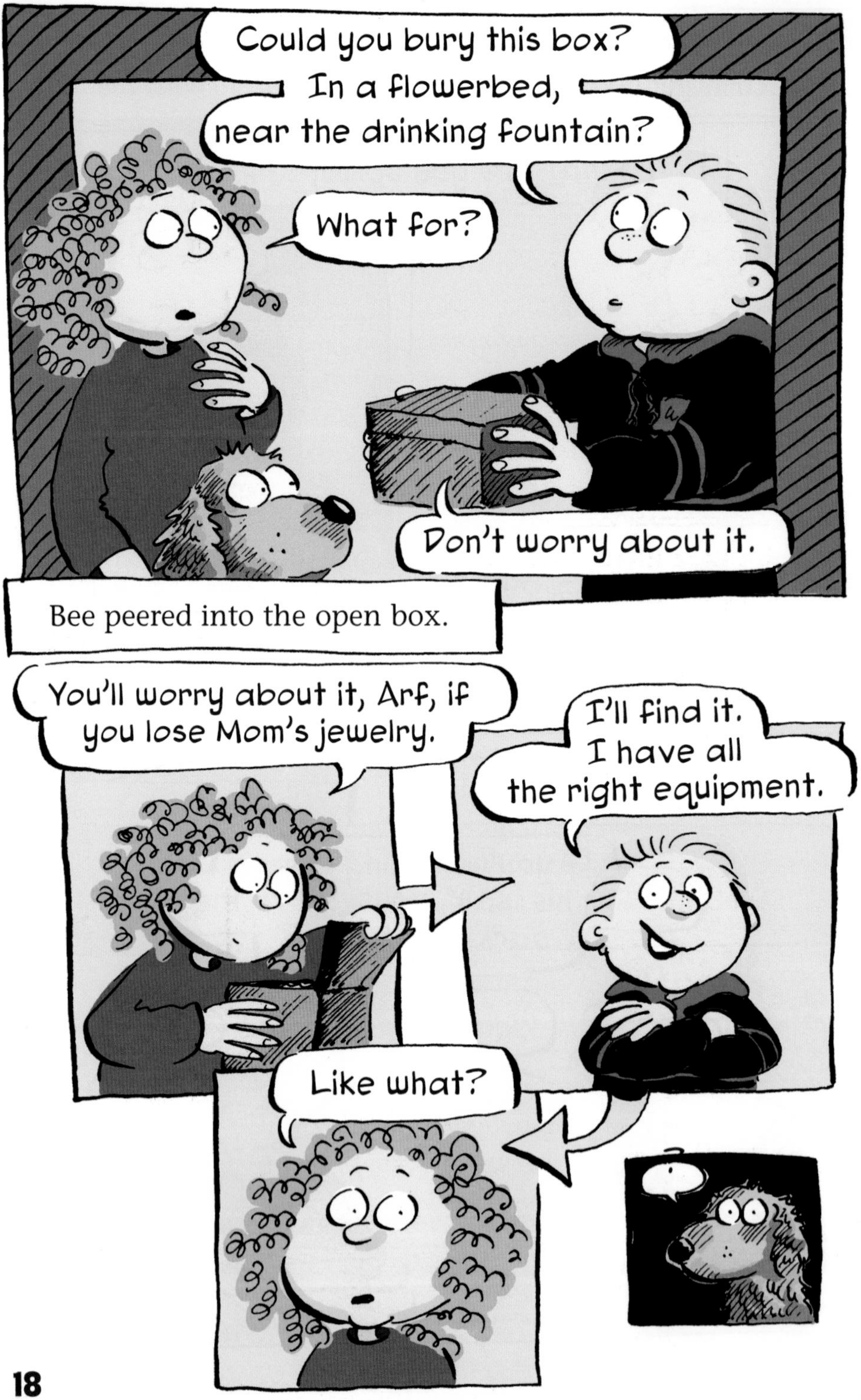
Could you bury this box?
In a flowerbed,
near the drinking fountain?
What for?
Don't worry about it.
Bee peered into the open box.
You'll worry about it, Arf, if you lose Mom's jewelry.
I'll find it. I have all the right equipment.
Like what?

Arf had to tell Bee everything. He told her about his bet with Gloria.

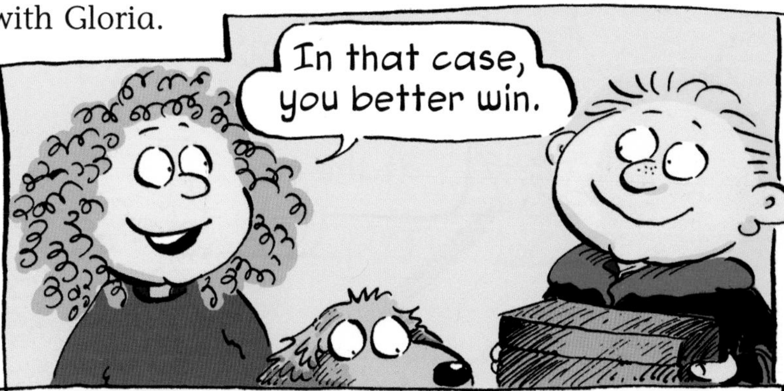
In that case, you better win.

Bee went back to her bedroom and came out a moment later holding a sheet of paper.

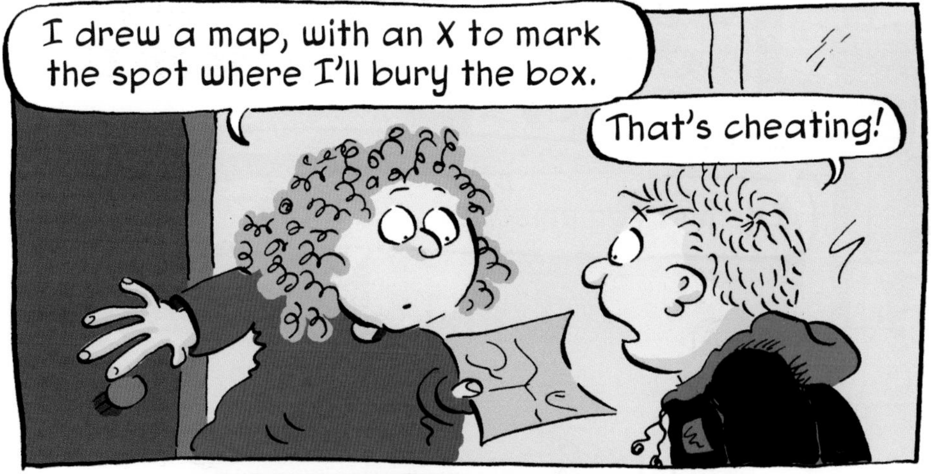
I drew a map, with an X to mark the spot where I'll bury the box.
That's cheating!

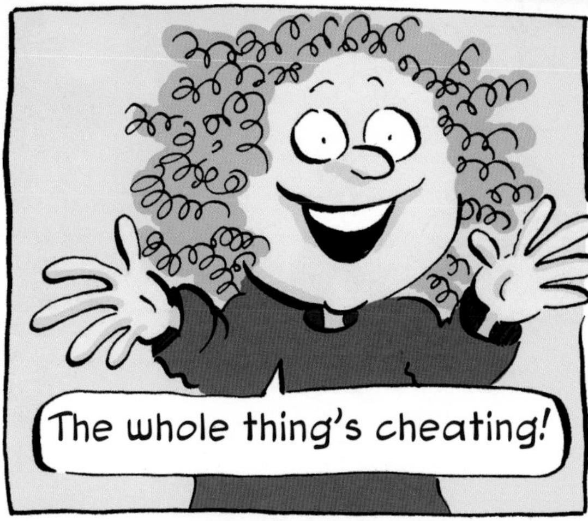
The whole thing's cheating!

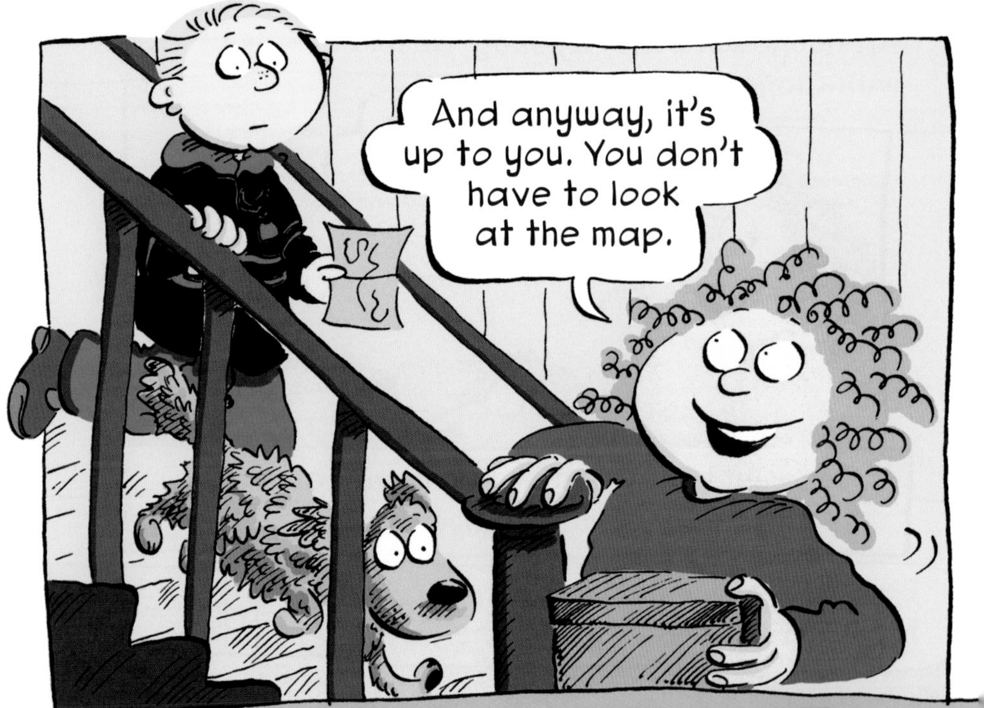
And anyway, it's up to you. You don't have to look at the map.
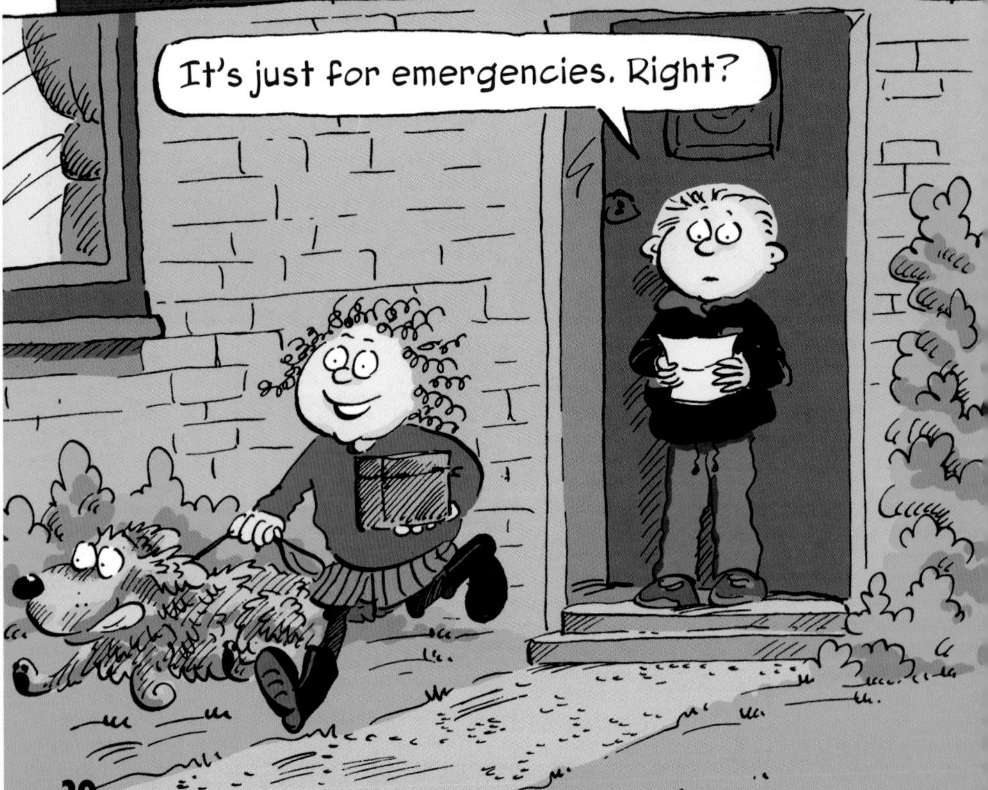
It's just for emergencies. Right?

# CHAPTER THREE

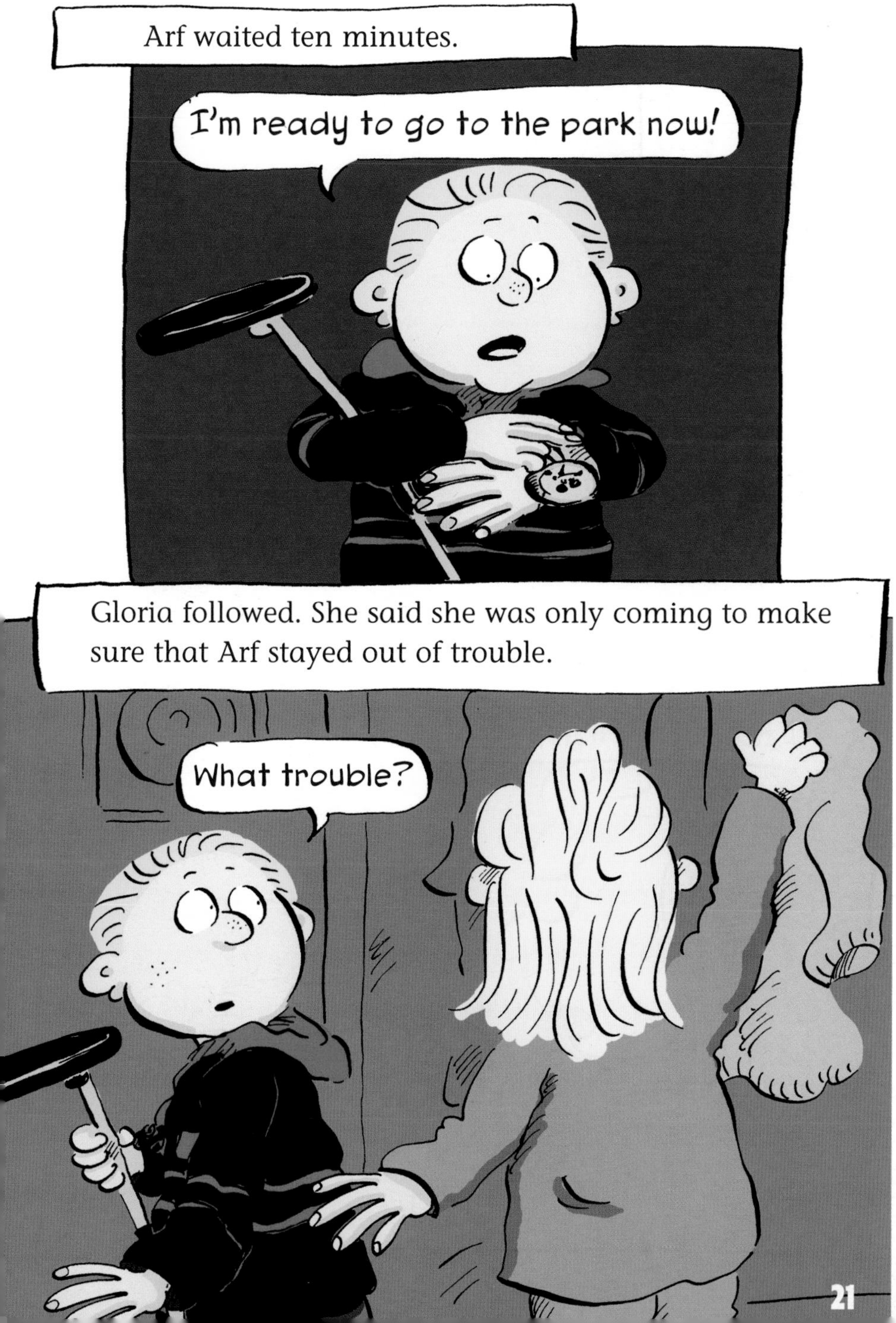
Arf waited ten minutes.
I'm ready to go to the park now!
Gloria followed. She said she was only coming to make sure that Arf stayed out of trouble.
What trouble?

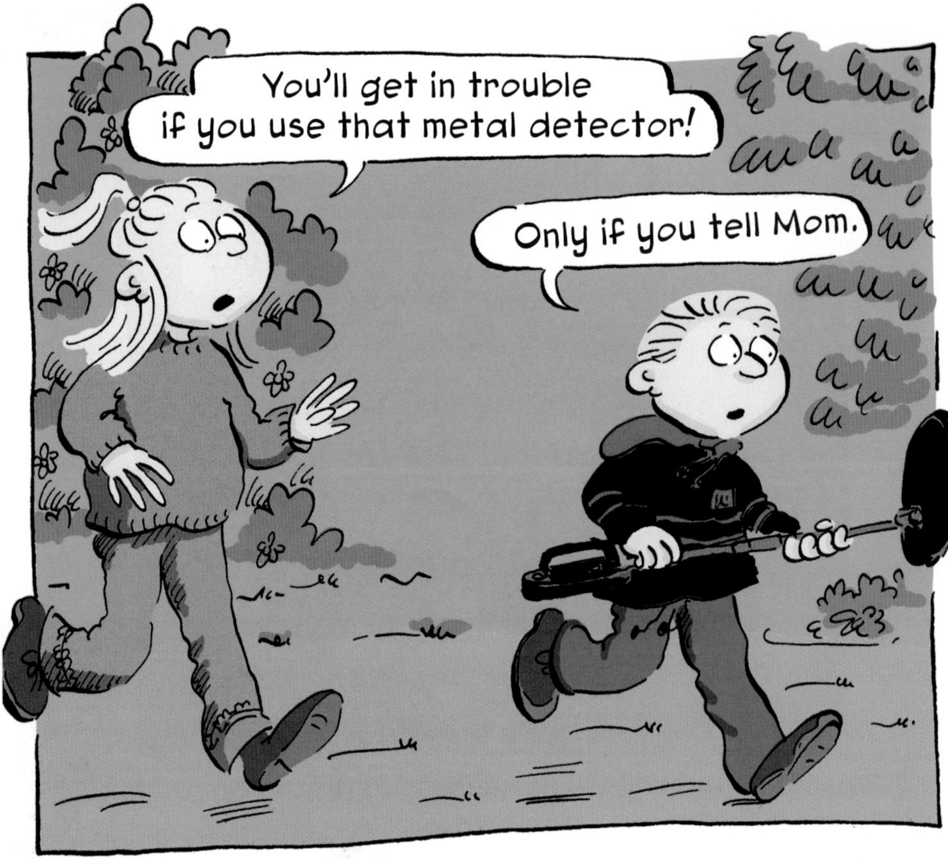
You'll get in trouble if you use that metal detector!
Only if you tell Mom.

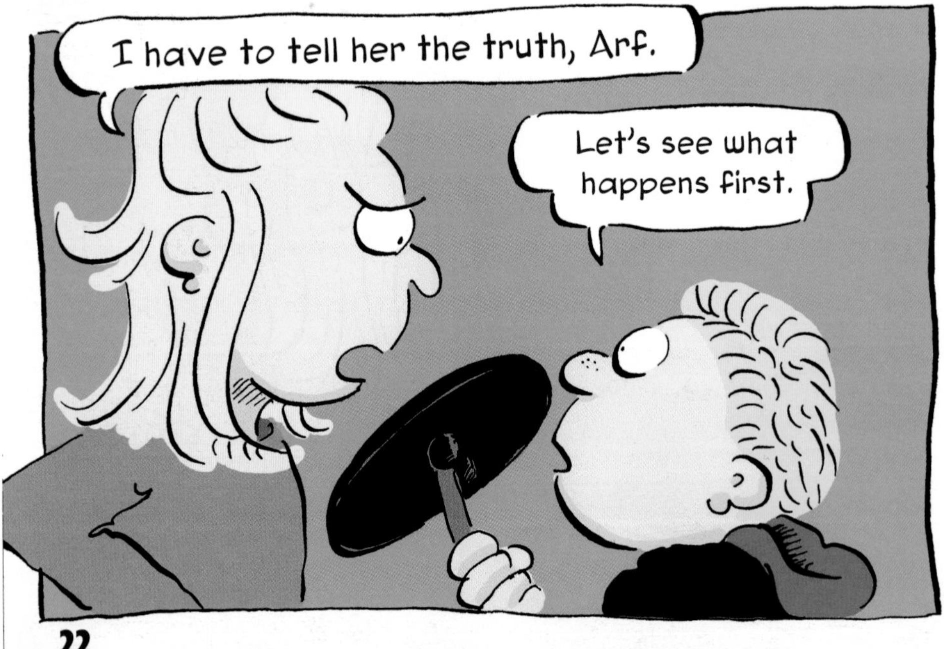
I have to tell her the truth, Arf.
Let's see what happens first.

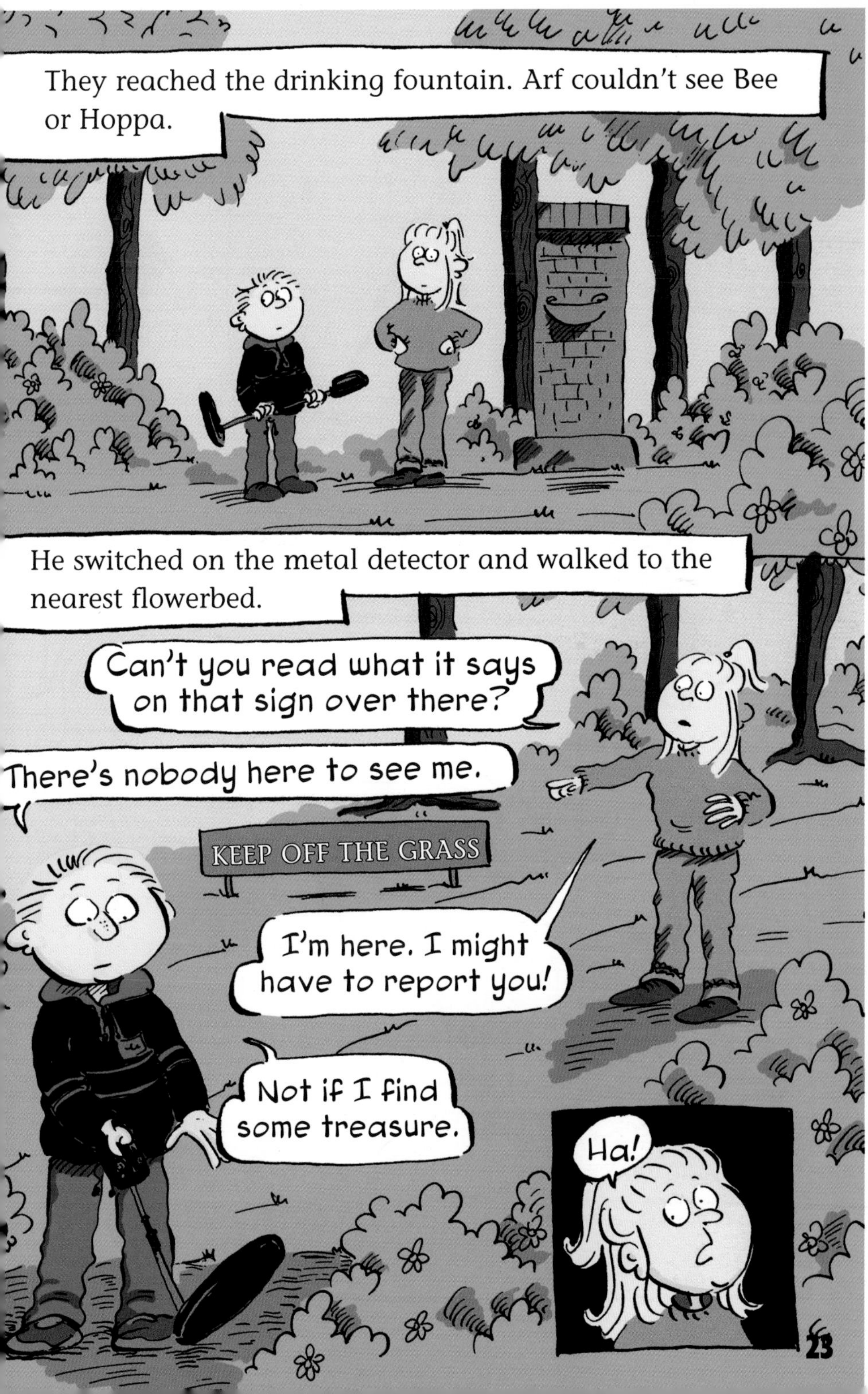
They reached the drinking fountain. Arf couldn't see Bee or Hoppa.
He switched on the metal detector and walked to the nearest flowerbed.
Can't you read what it says on that sign over there?
There's nobody here to see me.
KEEP OFF THE GRASS
I'm here. I might have to report you!
Not if I find some treasure.
Ha!

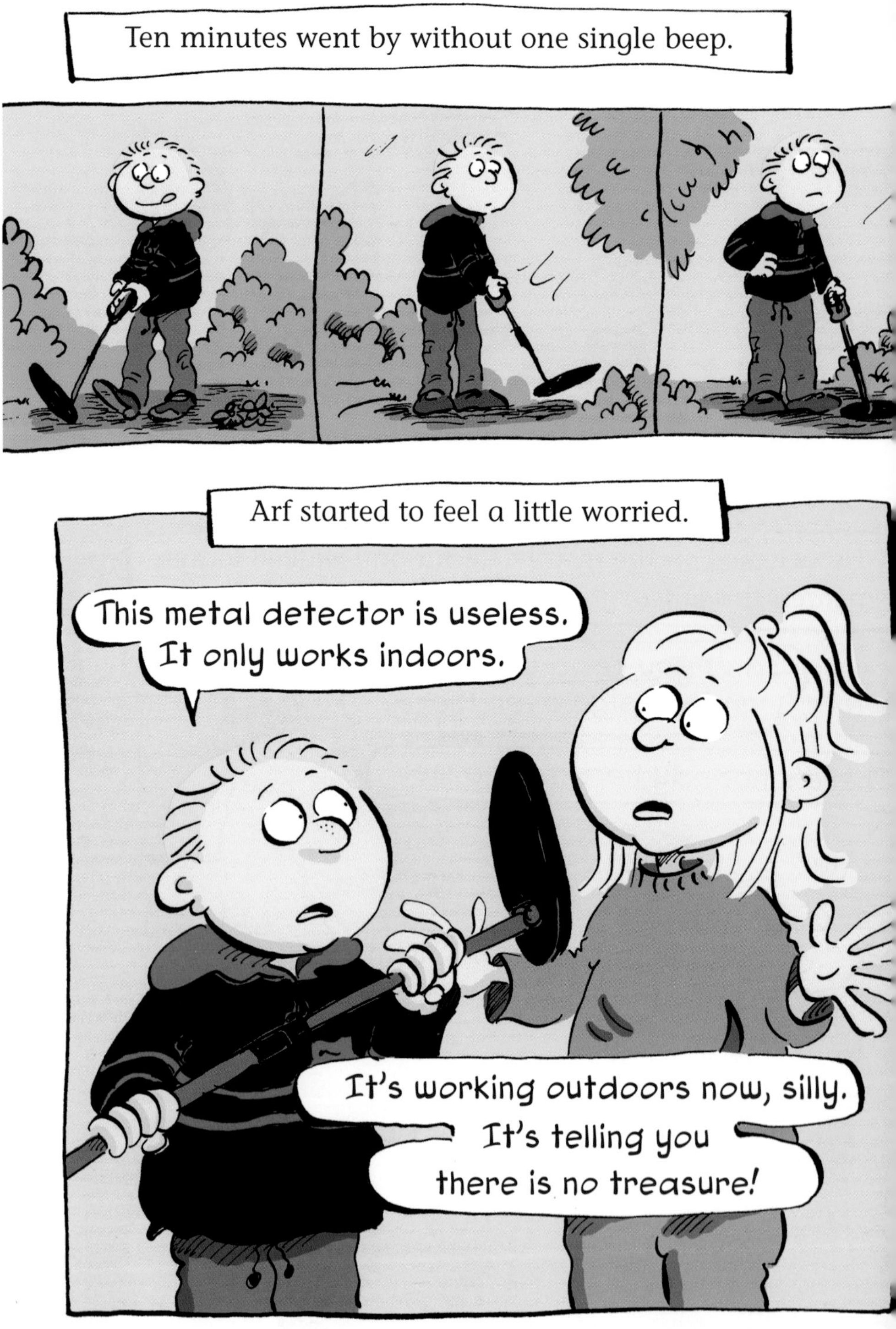
Ten minutes went by without one single beep.
Arf started to feel a little worried.
This metal detector is useless. It only works indoors.
It's working outdoors now, silly. It's telling you there is no treasure!

Ten more minutes went by. Gloria paced up and down.

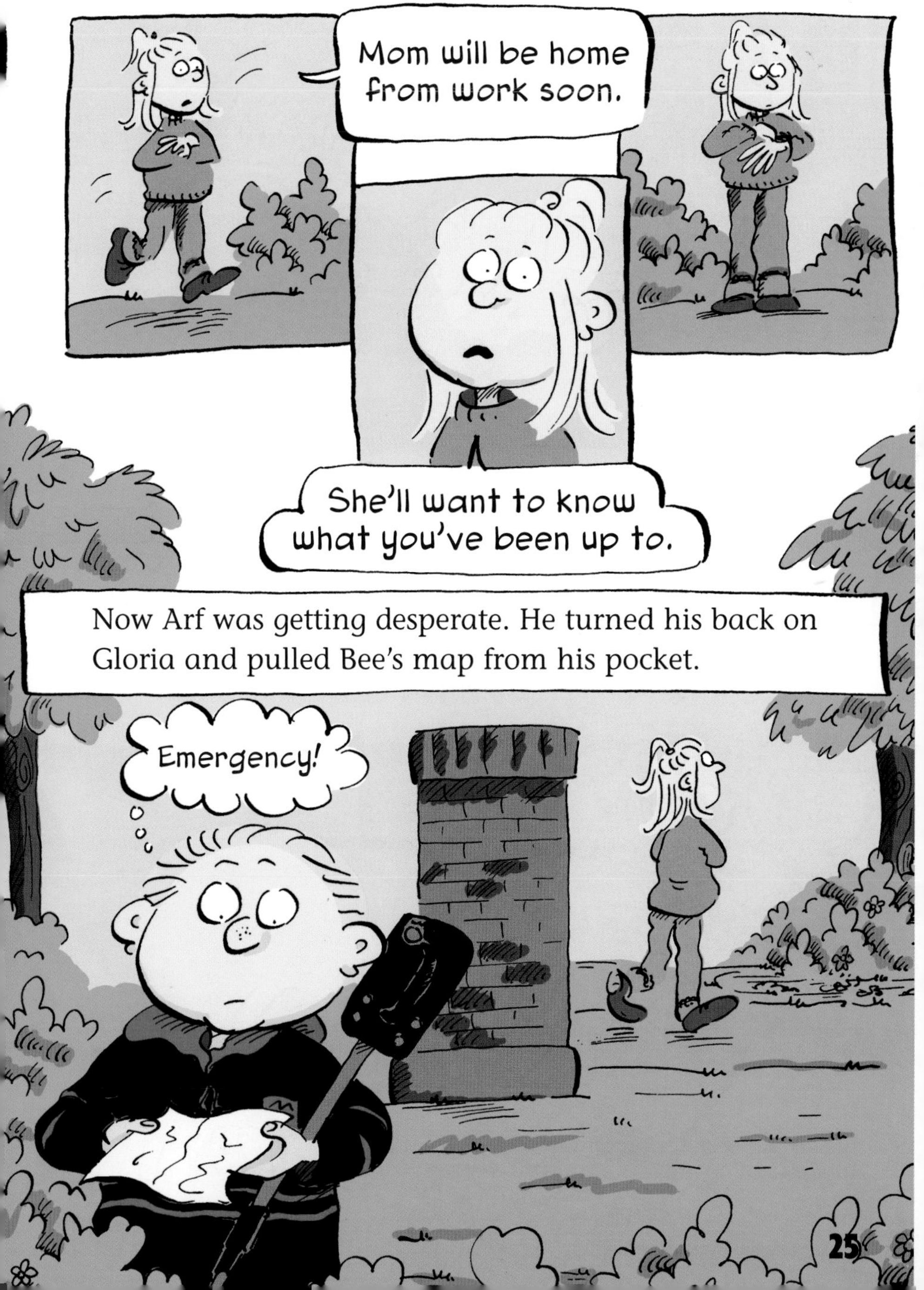
Mom will be home from work soon.
She'll want to know what you've been up to.
Now Arf was getting desperate. He turned his back on Gloria and pulled Bee's map from his pocket.
Emergency!

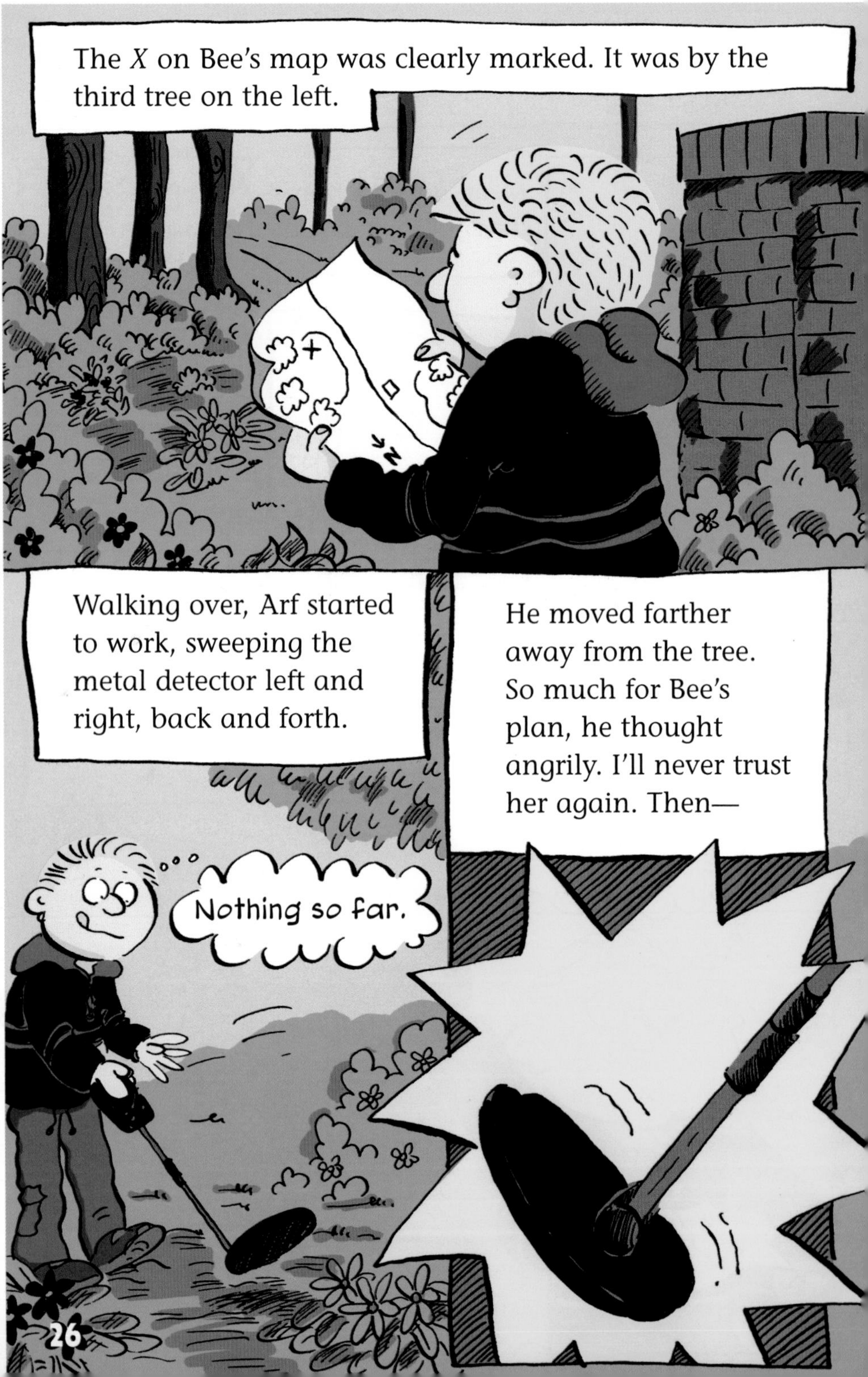
The *X* on Bee's map was clearly marked. It was by the third tree on the left.
Walking over, Arf started to work, sweeping the metal detector left and right, back and forth.
Nothing so far.
He moved farther away from the tree. So much for Bee's plan, he thought angrily. I'll never trust her again. Then—

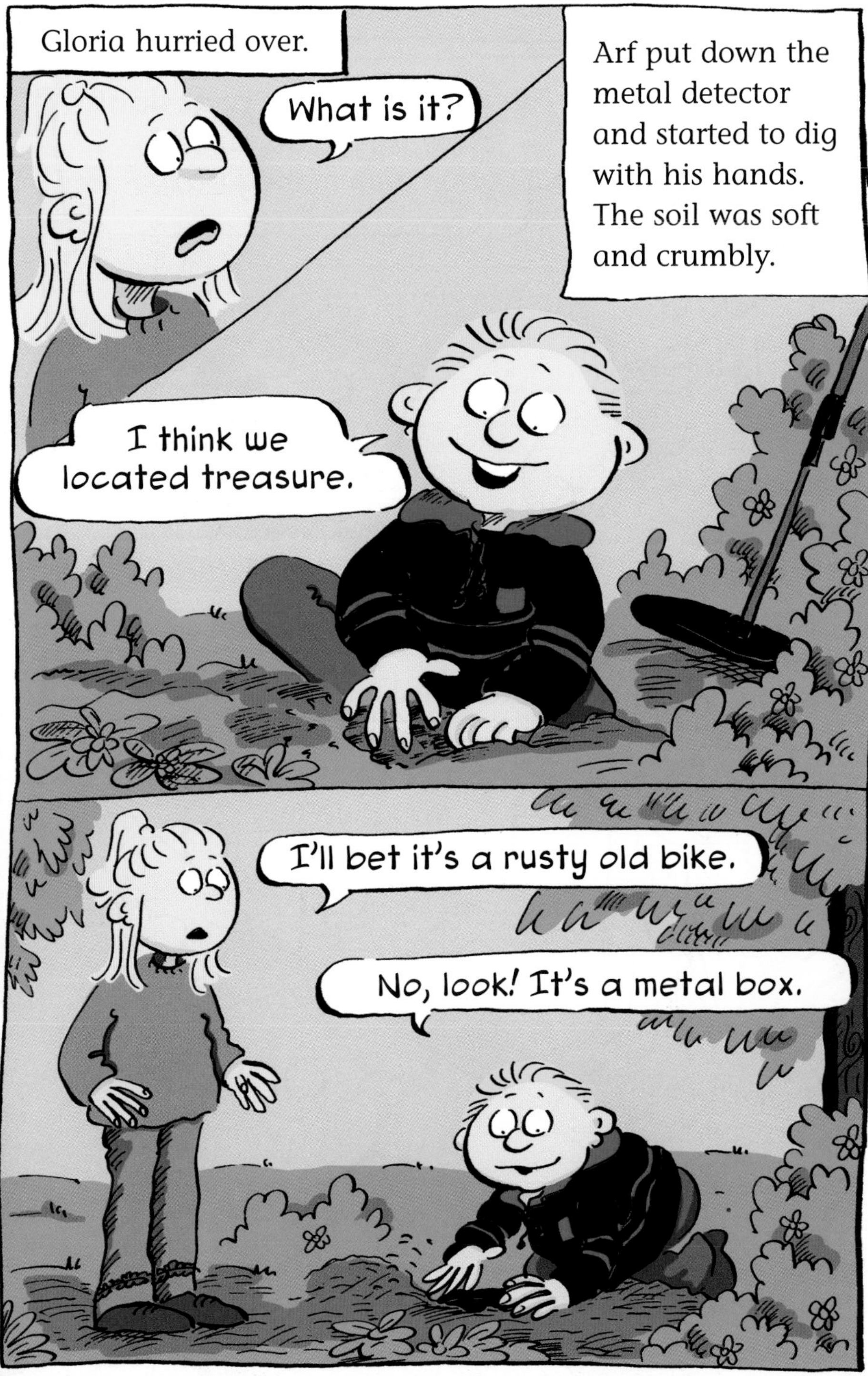
Gloria hurried over.
What is it?
Arf put down the metal detector and started to dig with his hands. The soil was soft and crumbly.
I think we located treasure.
I'll bet it's a rusty old bike.
No, look! It's a metal box.

Gloria took one look and planted her hands on her hips.

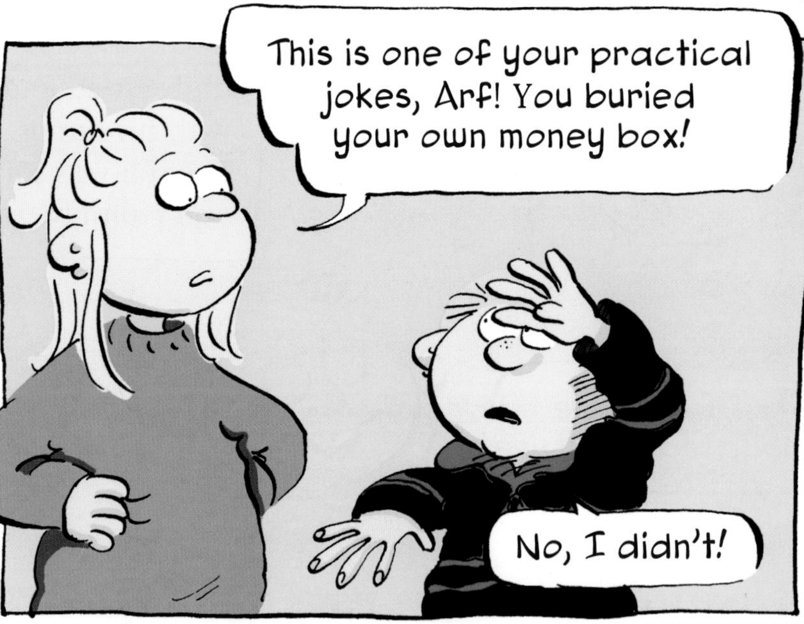
This is one of your practical jokes, Arf! You buried your own money box!
No, I didn't!

Gloria marched off and called over her shoulder.

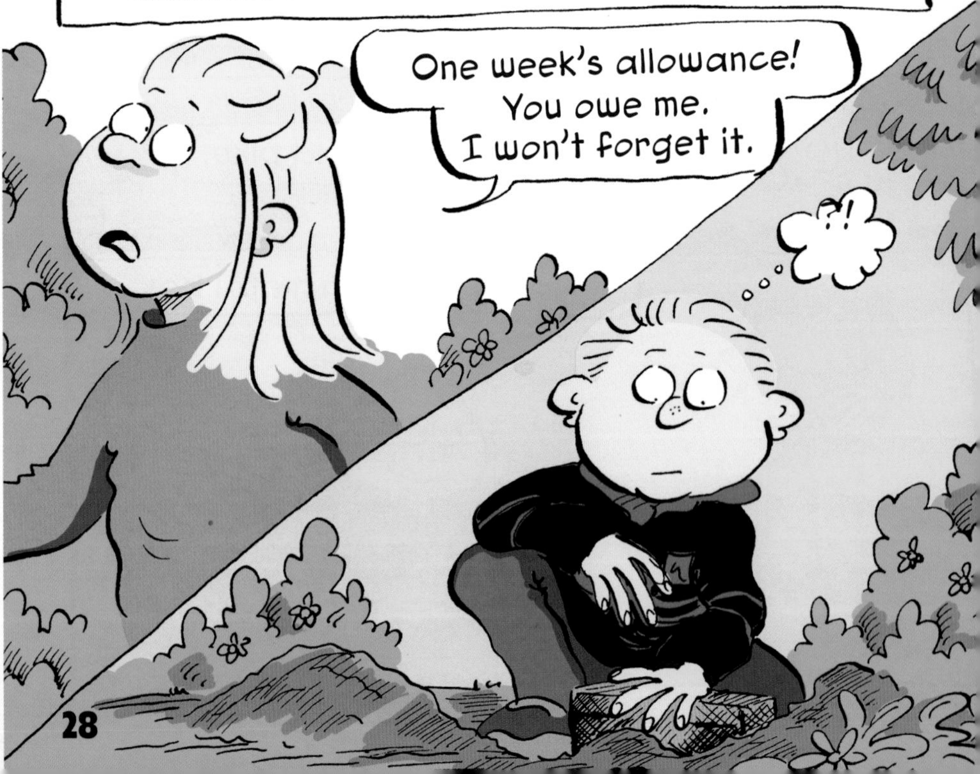
One week's allowance! You owe me. I won't forget it.
?!

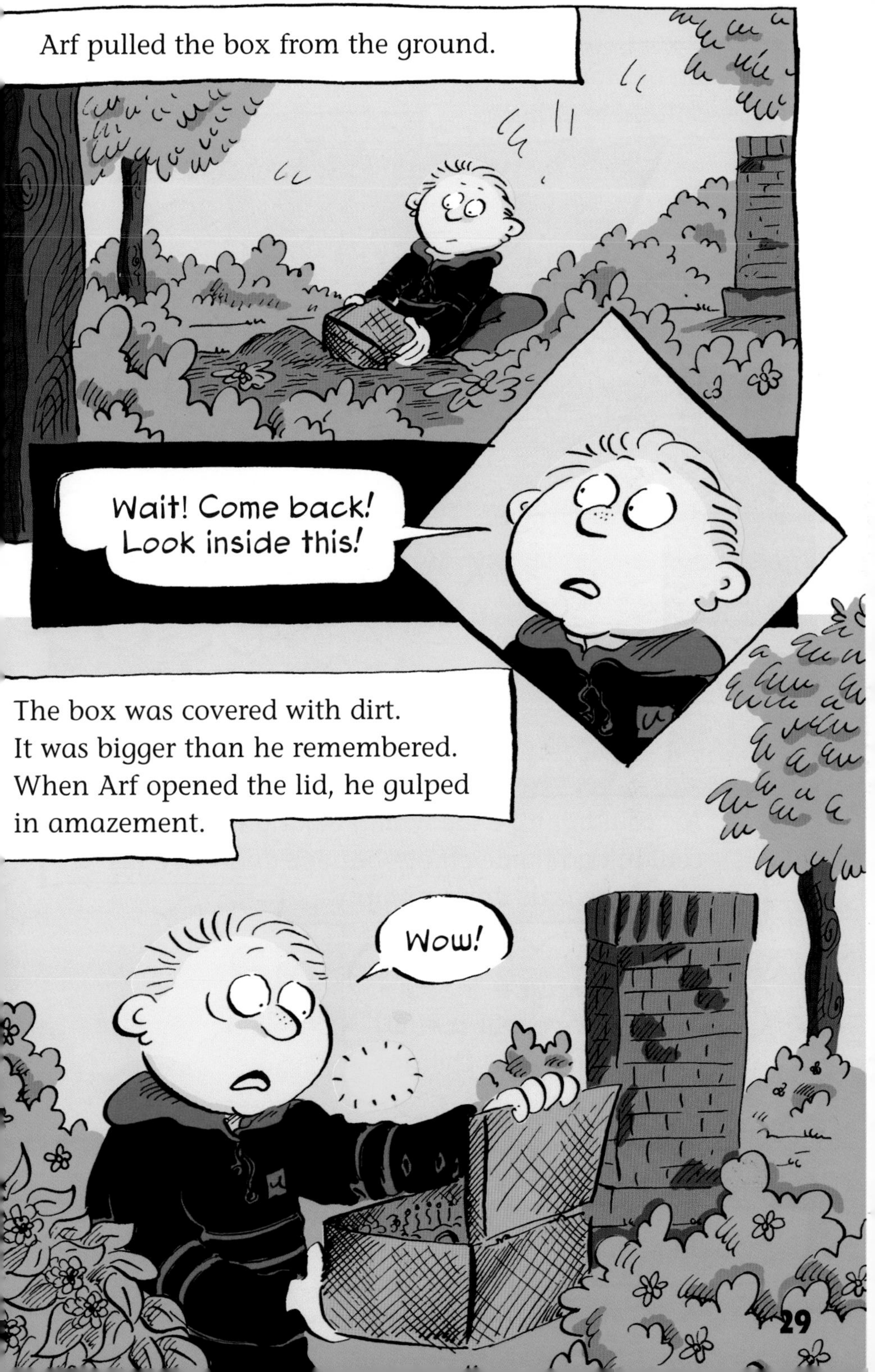
Arf pulled the box from the ground.
Wait! Come back! Look inside this!
The box was covered with dirt. It was bigger than he remembered. When Arf opened the lid, he gulped in amazement.
Wow!

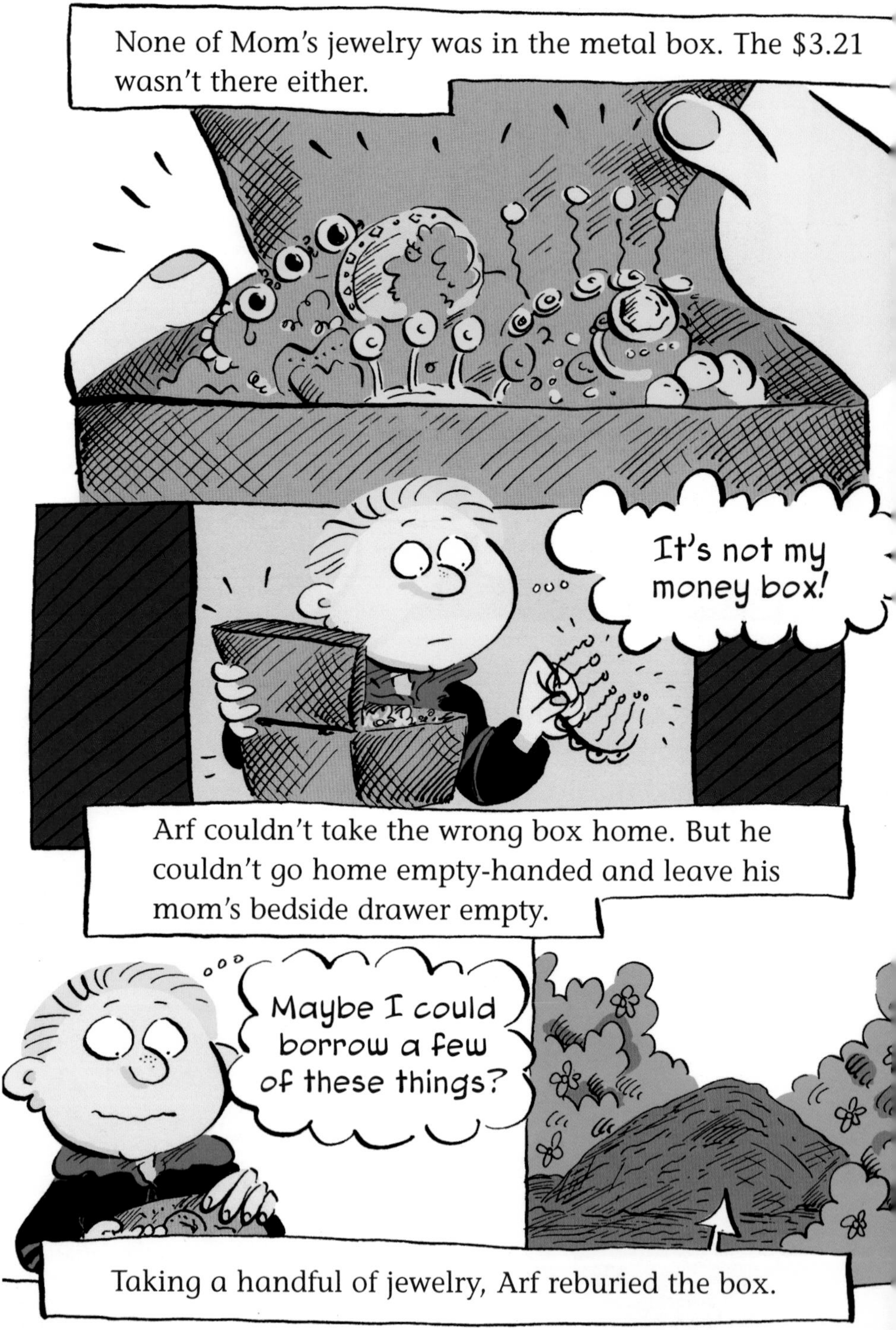
None of Mom's jewelry was in the metal box. The $3.21 wasn't there either.
It's not my money box!
Arf couldn't take the wrong box home. But he couldn't go home empty-handed and leave his mom's bedside drawer empty.
Maybe I could borrow a few of these things?
Taking a handful of jewelry, Arf reburied the box.

# CHAPTER FOUR

Back home, he shoved the jewelry into Mom's bedside drawer. He hoped she wouldn't look closely and notice that it wasn't her own.

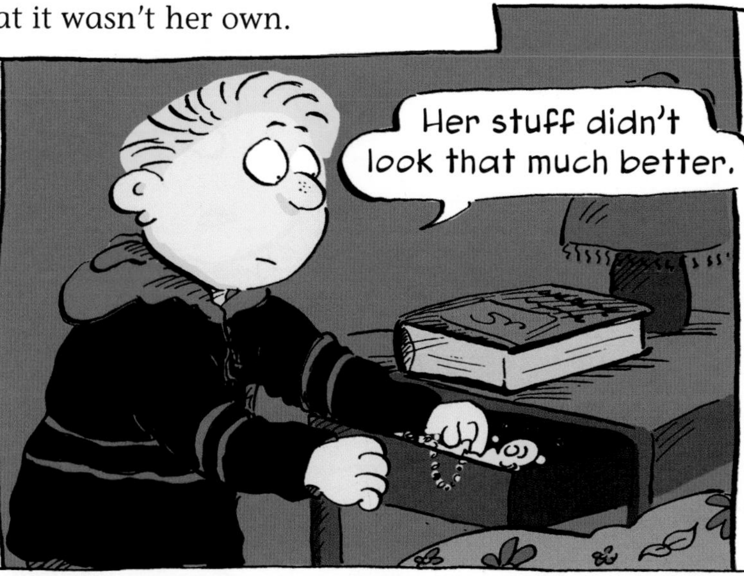
Her stuff didn't look that much better.

But where was Mom's stuff? Arf needed to talk to Bee. She was now back from her walk with Hoppa.

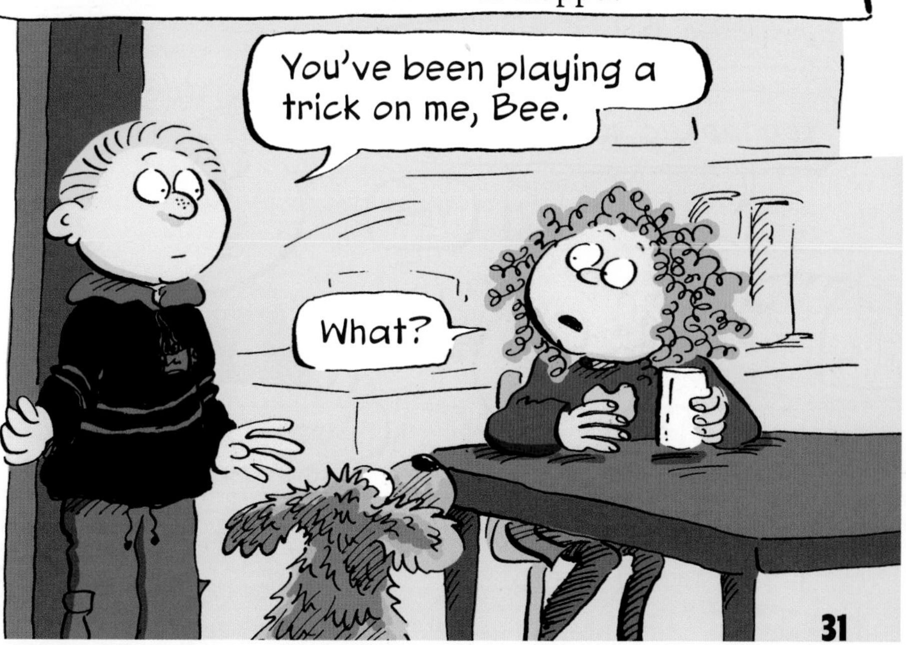
You've been playing a trick on me, Bee.
What?

She didn't look sorry. But when Arf told her about finding the box full of jewelry, she did look very puzzled.

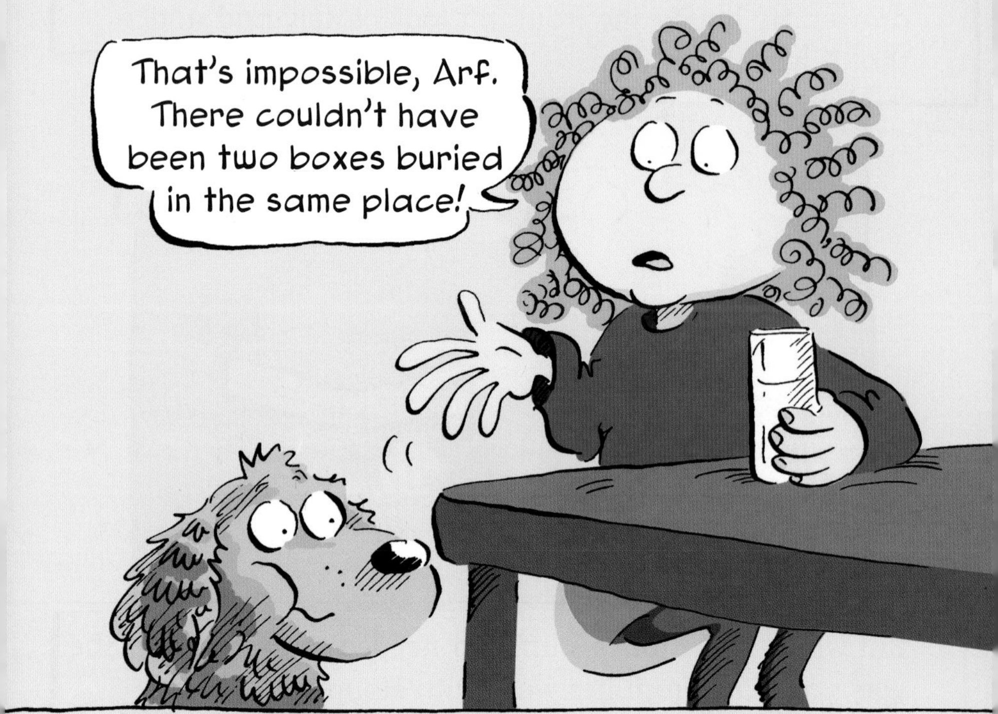
That's impossible, Arf. There couldn't have been two boxes buried in the same place!

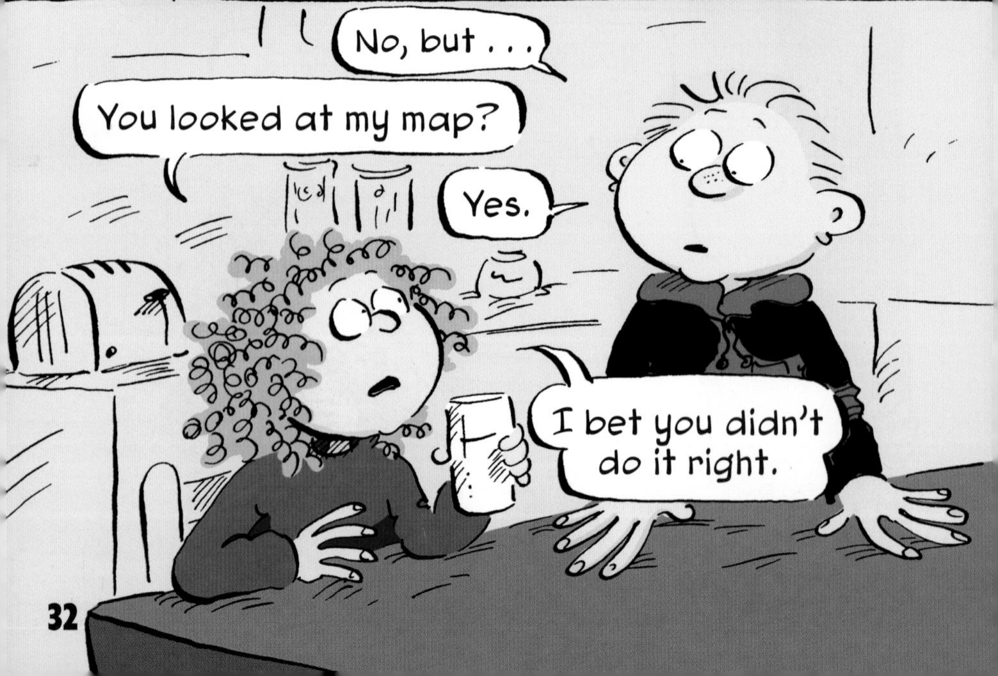
You looked at my map?
Yes.
No, but . . .
I bet you didn't do it right.

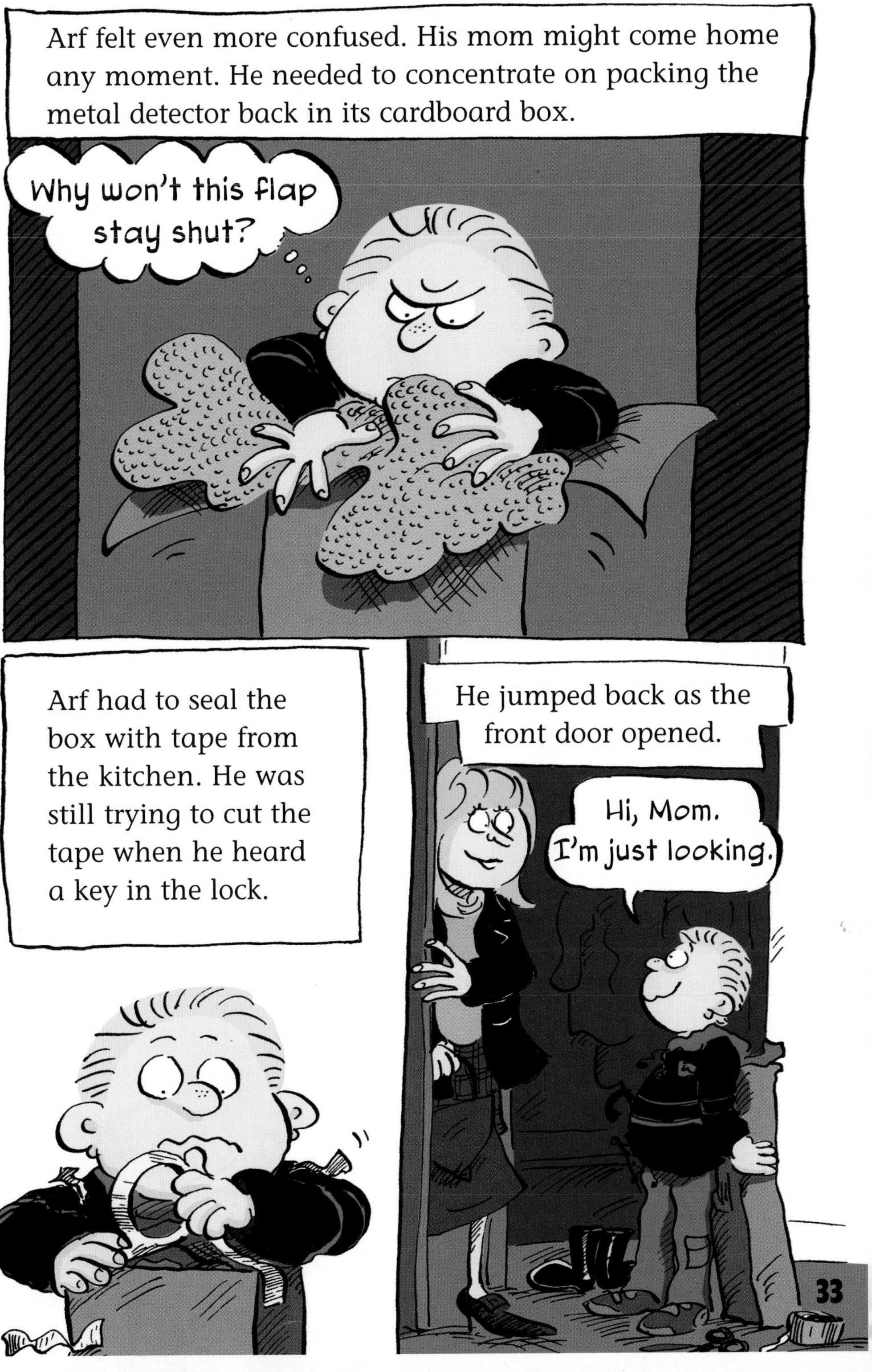
Arf felt even more confused. His mom might come home any moment. He needed to concentrate on packing the metal detector back in its cardboard box.
Why won't this flap stay shut?
Arf had to seal the box with tape from the kitchen. He was still trying to cut the tape when he heard a key in the lock.
He jumped back as the front door opened.
Hi, Mom. I'm just looking.

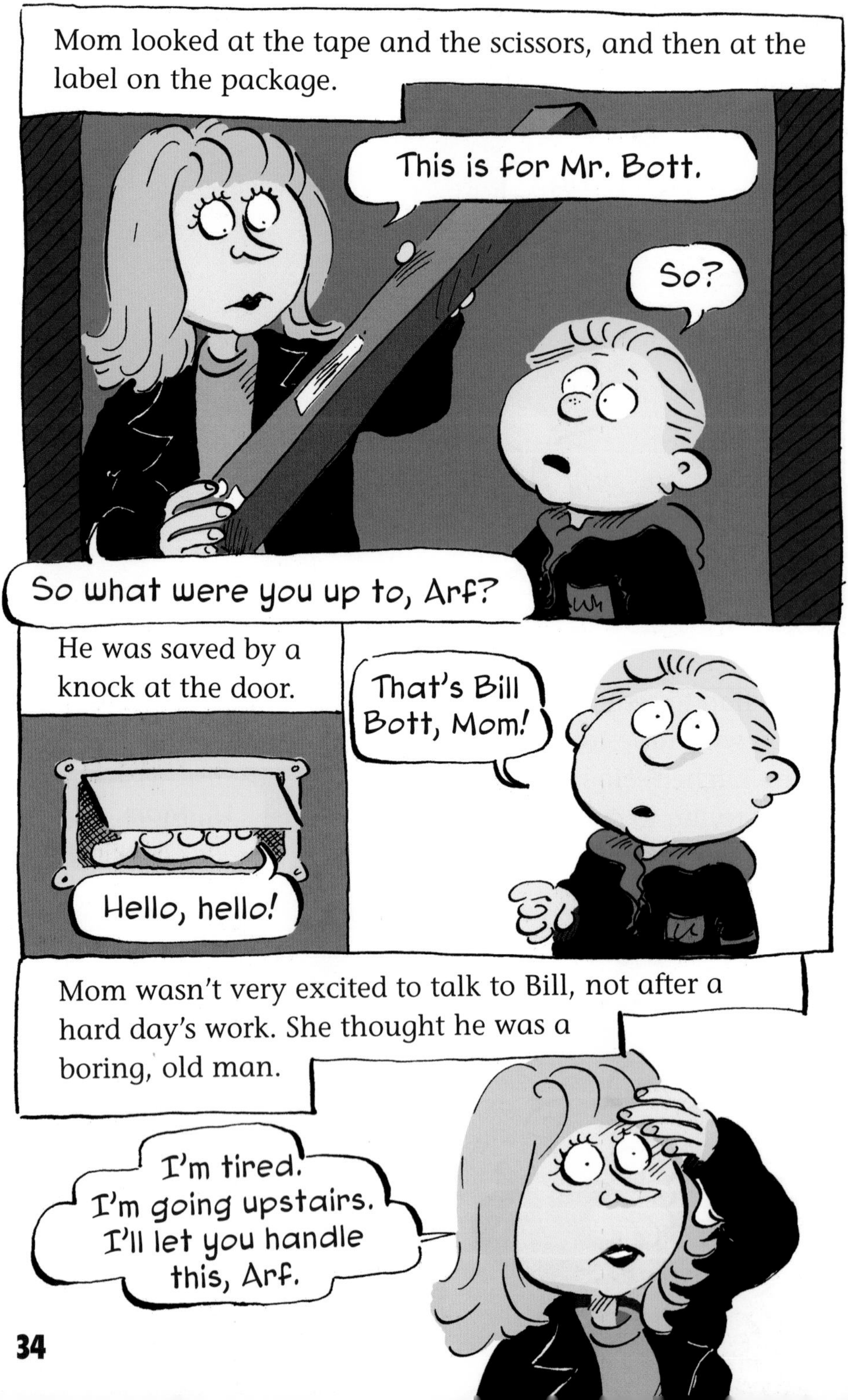
Mom looked at the tape and the scissors, and then at the label on the package.
This is for Mr. Bott.
So?
So what were you up to, Arf?
He was saved by a knock at the door.
Hello, hello!
That's Bill Bott, Mom!
Mom wasn't very excited to talk to Bill, not after a hard day's work. She thought he was a boring, old man.
I'm tired. I'm going upstairs. I'll let you handle this, Arf.

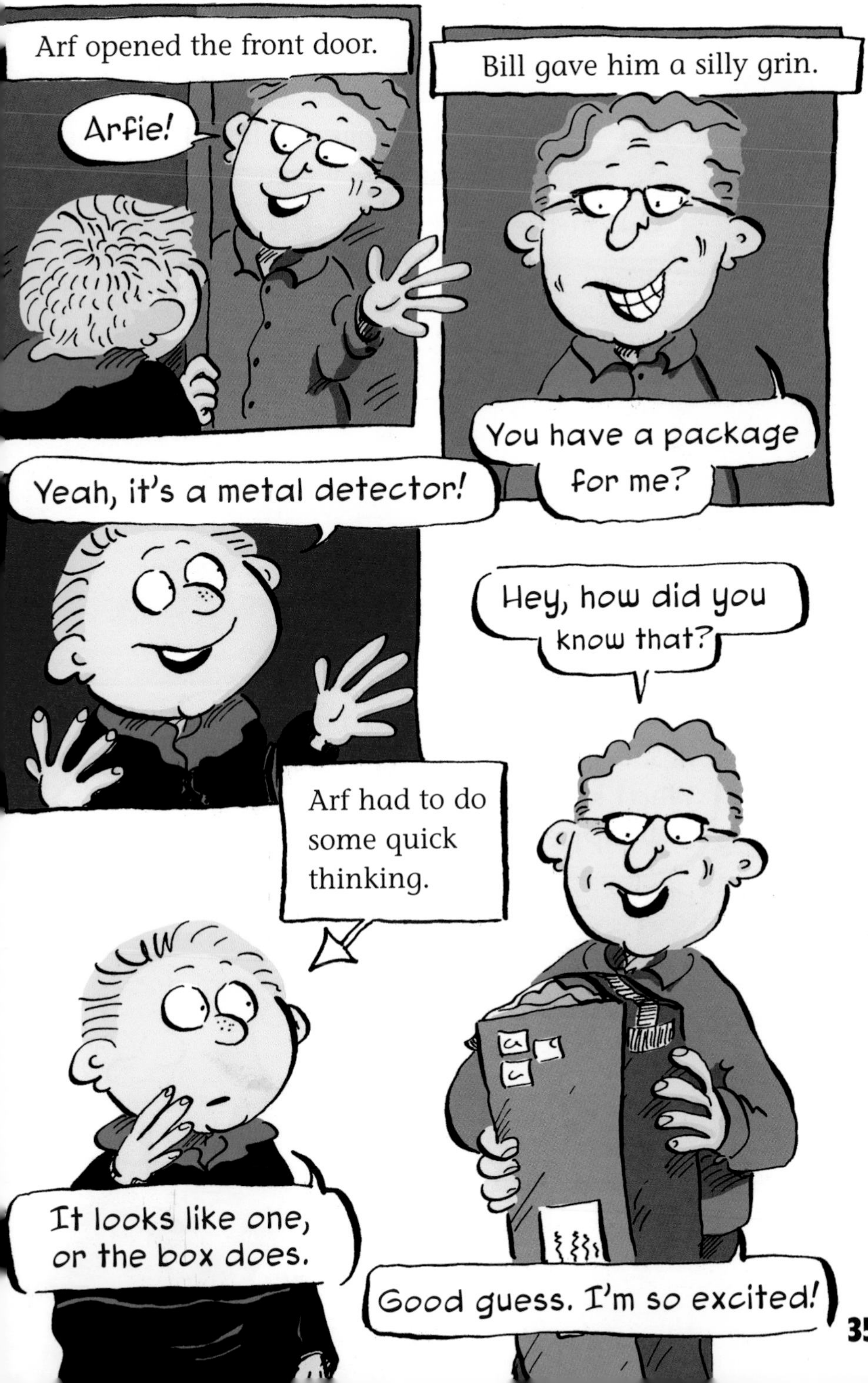
Arf opened the front door.
Arfie!
Bill gave him a silly grin.
You have a package for me?
Yeah, it's a metal detector!
Hey, how did you know that?
Arf had to do some quick thinking.
It looks like one, or the box does.
Good guess. I'm so excited!

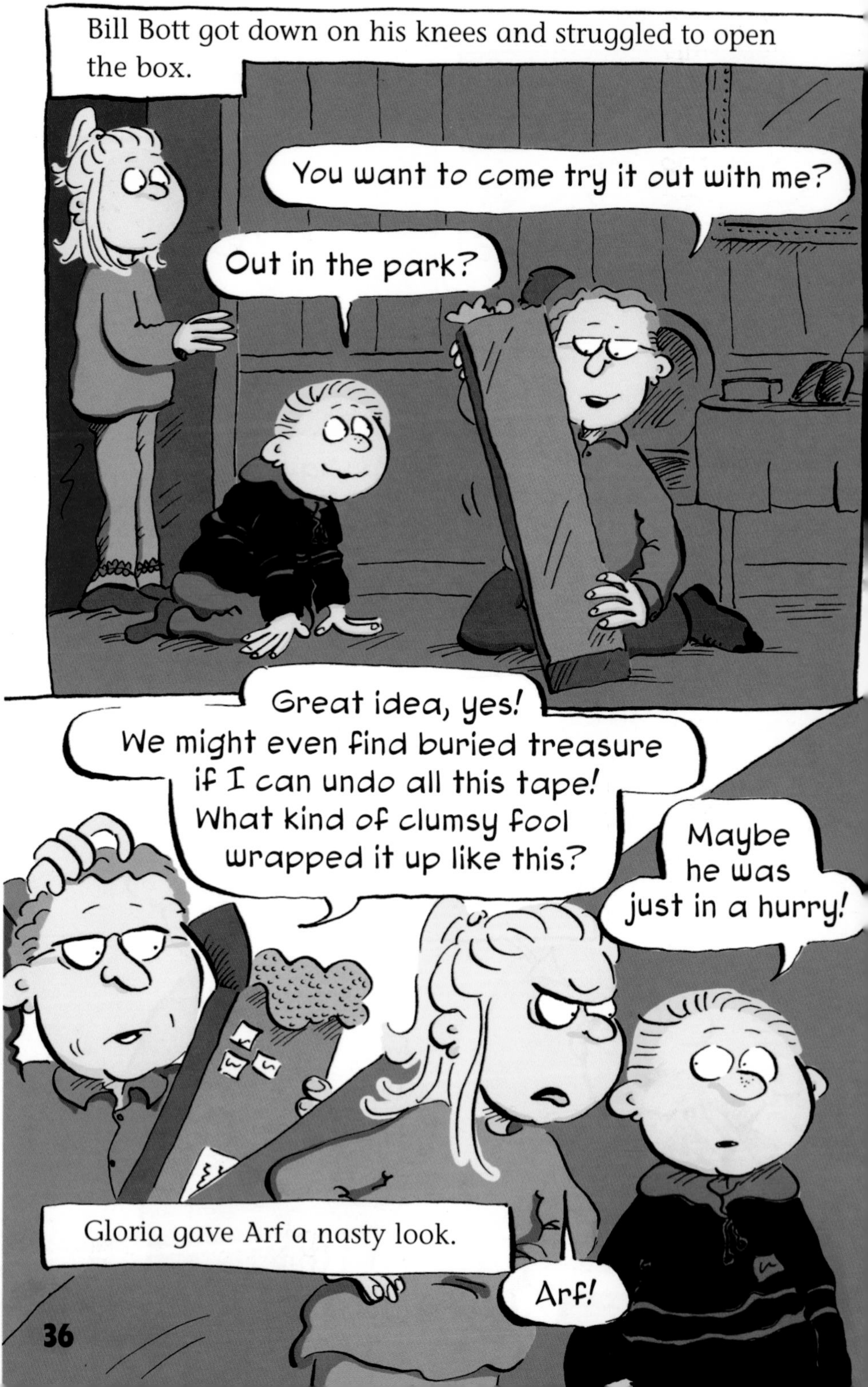
Bill Bott got down on his knees and struggled to open the box.
You want to come try it out with me?
Out in the park?
Great idea, yes!
We might even find buried treasure if I can undo all this tape!
What kind of clumsy fool wrapped it up like this?
Maybe he was just in a hurry!
Gloria gave Arf a nasty look.
Arf!

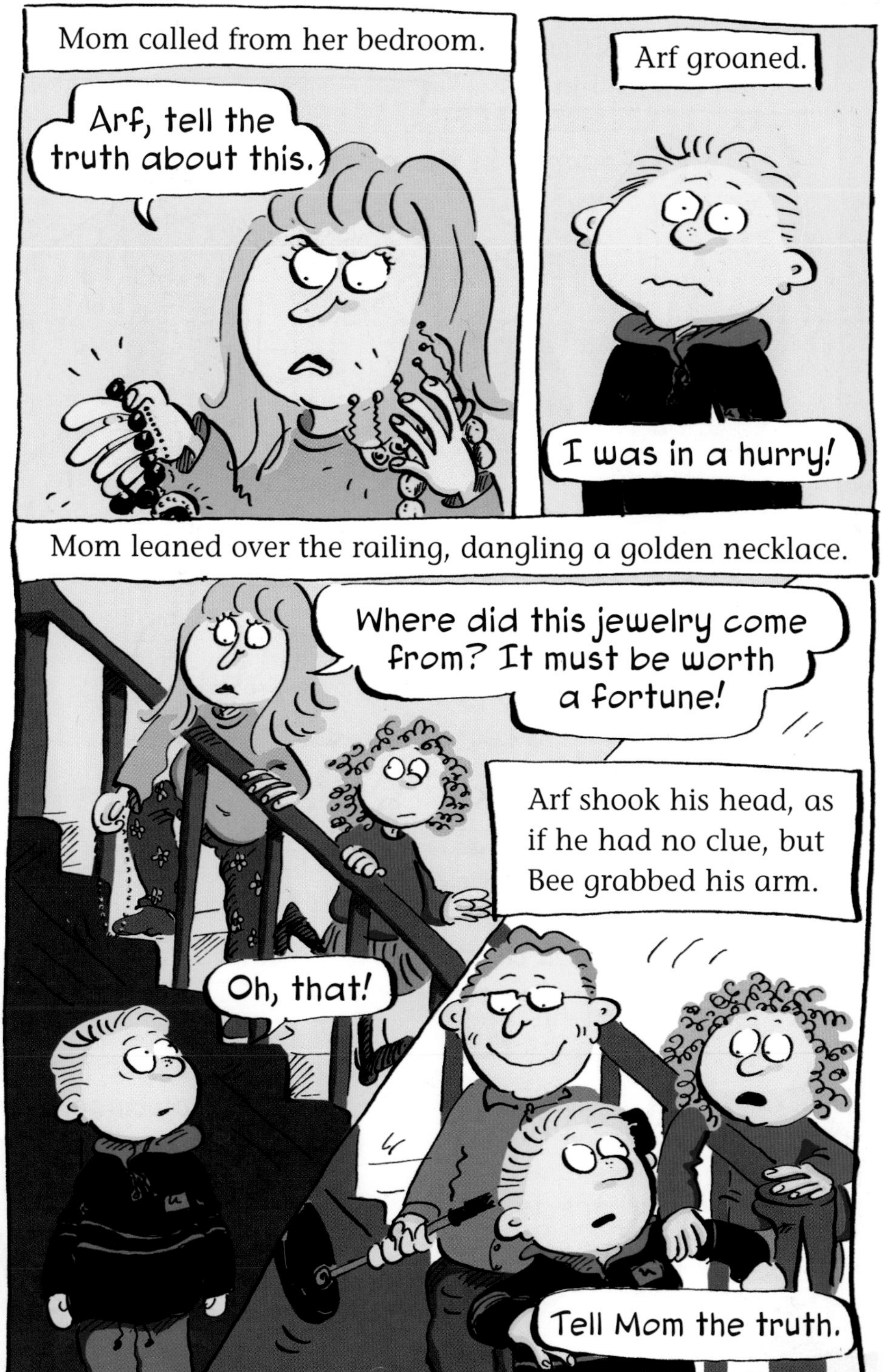
Mom called from her bedroom.
Arf, tell the truth about this.
Arf groaned.
I was in a hurry!
Mom leaned over the railing, dangling a golden necklace.
Where did this jewelry come from? It must be worth a fortune!
Arf shook his head, as if he had no clue, but Bee grabbed his arm.
Oh, that!
Tell Mom the truth.

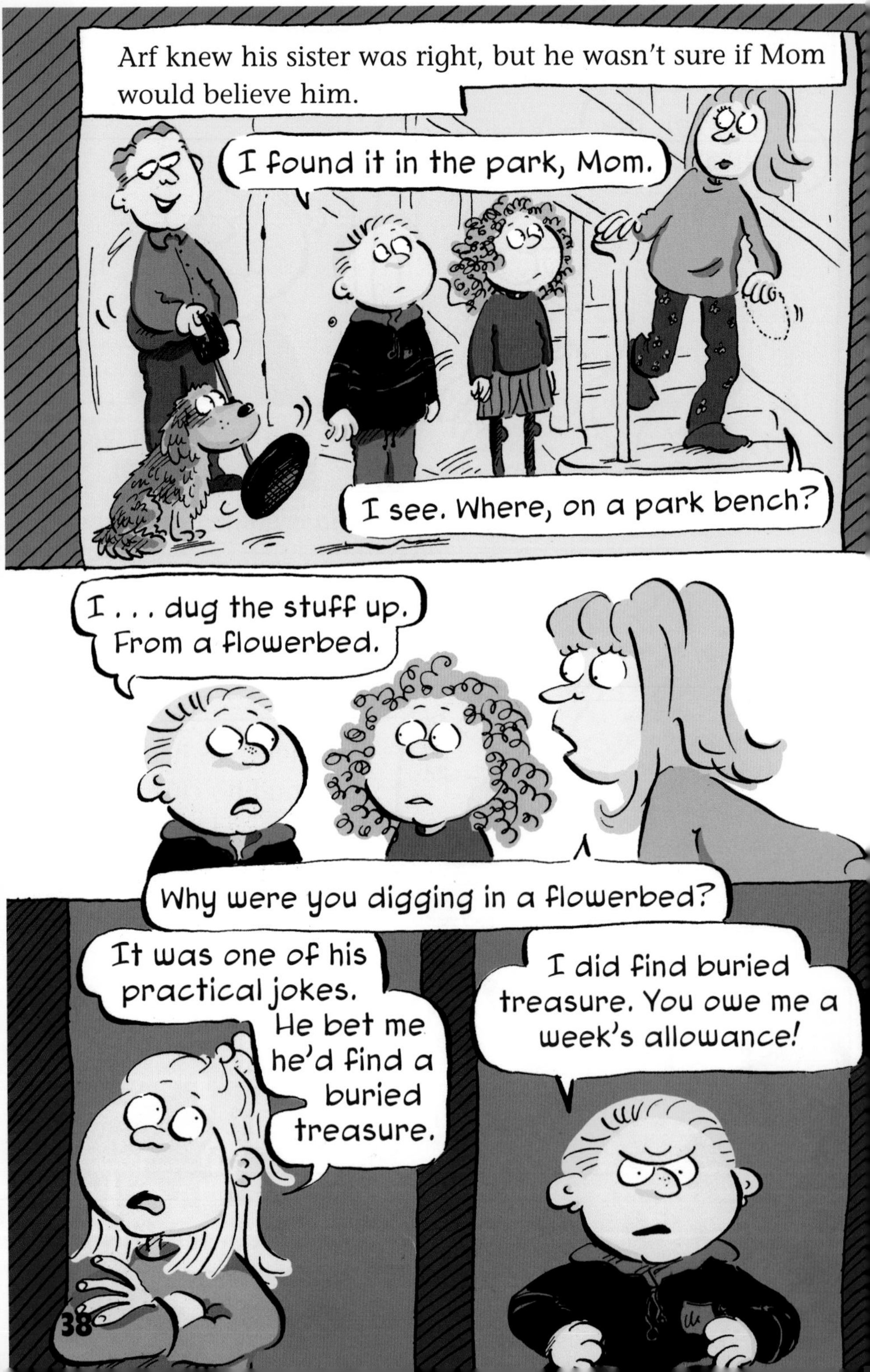

Arf knew his sister was right, but he wasn't sure if Mom would believe him.
I found it in the park, Mom.
I see. Where, on a park bench?
I . . . dug the stuff up. From a flowerbed.
Why were you digging in a flowerbed?
It was one of his practical jokes. He bet me he'd find a buried treasure.
I did find buried treasure. You owe me a week's allowance!

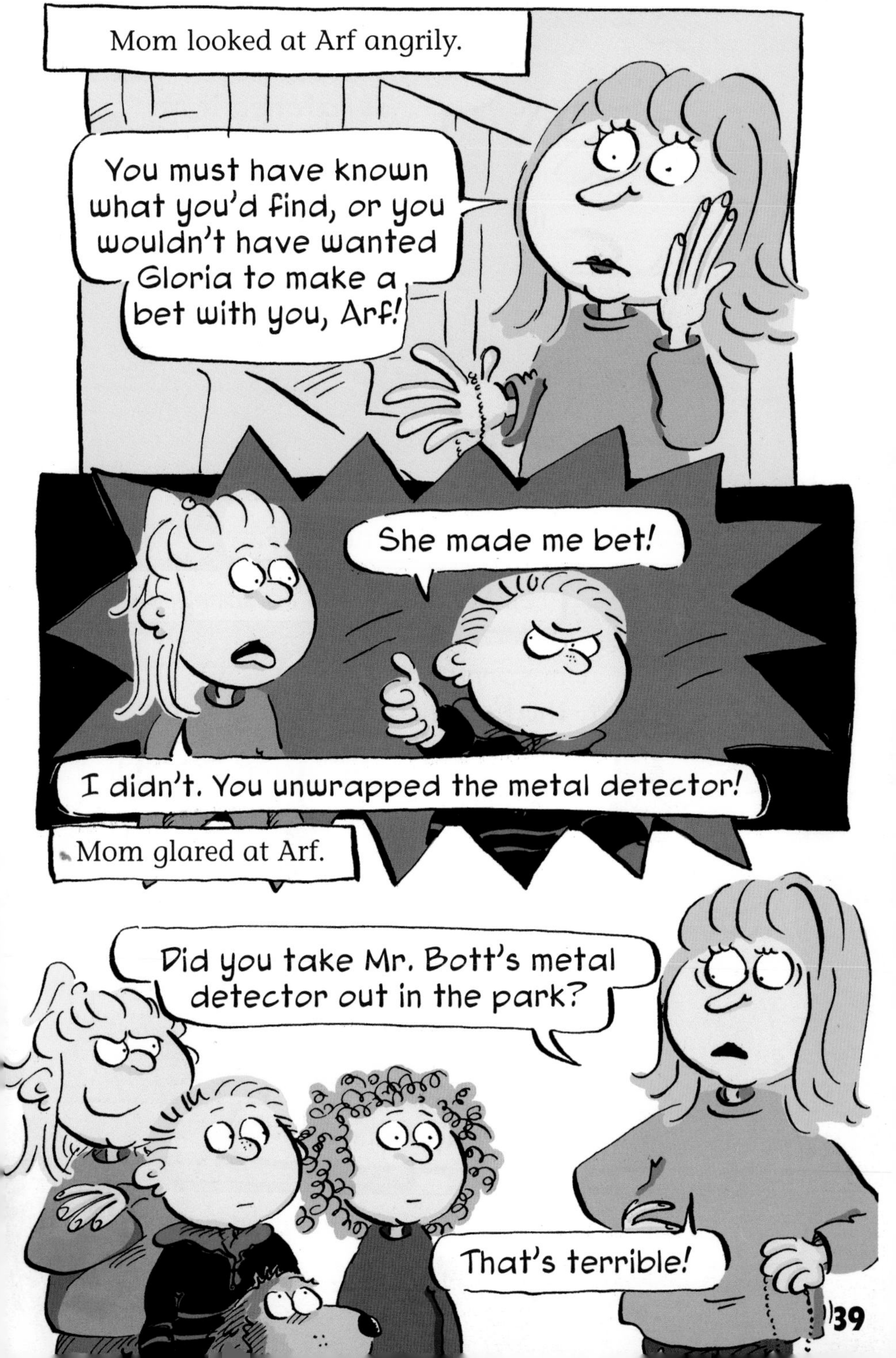
Mom looked at Arf angrily.
You must have known what you'd find, or you wouldn't have wanted Gloria to make a bet with you, Arf!
She made me bet!
I didn't. You unwrapped the metal detector!
Mom glared at Arf.
Did you take Mr. Bott's metal detector out in the park?
That's terrible!

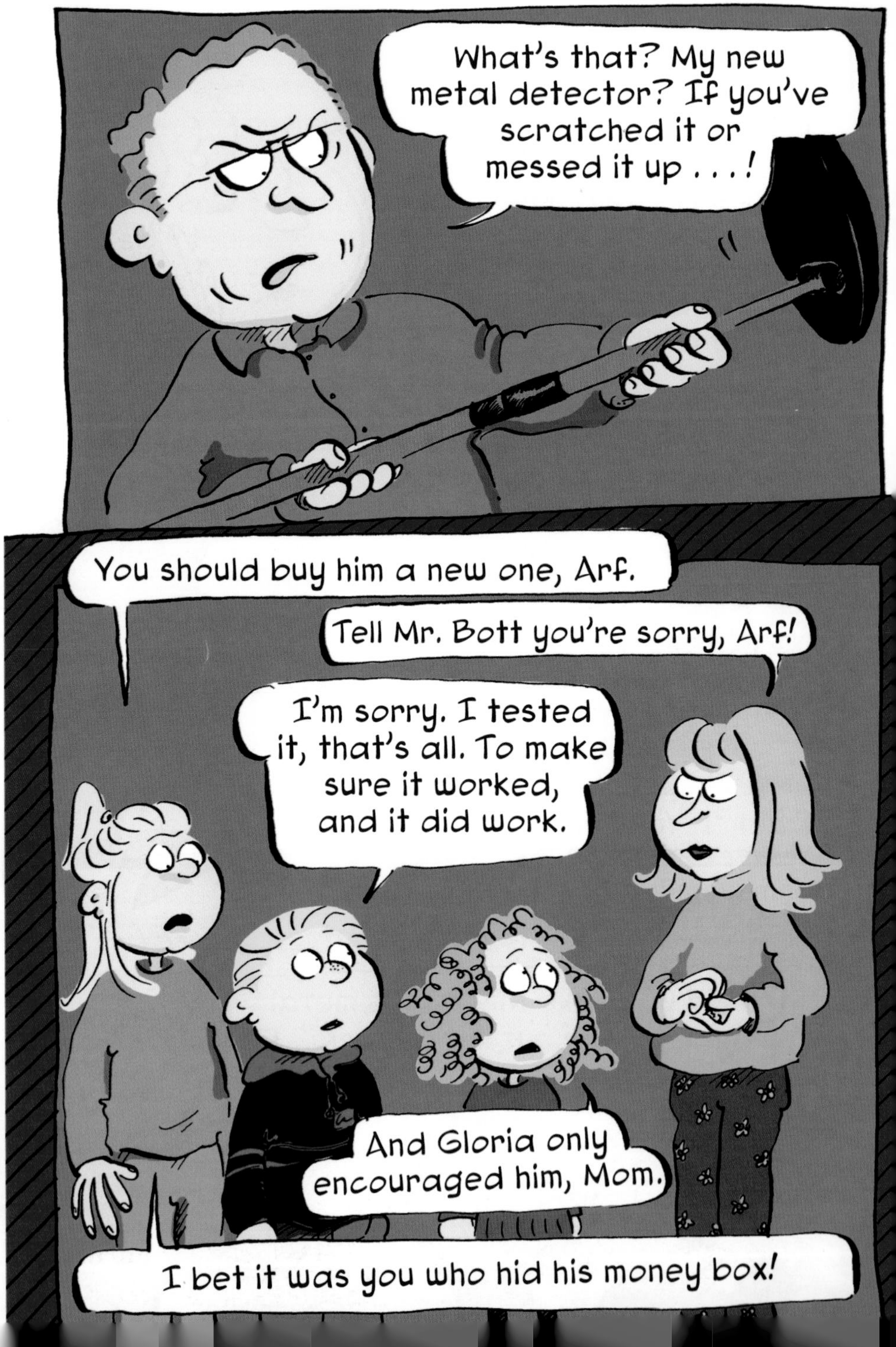
What's that? My new metal detector? If you've scratched it or messed it up . . . !
You should buy him a new one, Arf.
Tell Mr. Bott you're sorry, Arf!
I'm sorry. I tested it, that's all. To make sure it worked, and it did work.
And Gloria only encouraged him, Mom.
I bet it was you who hid his money box!

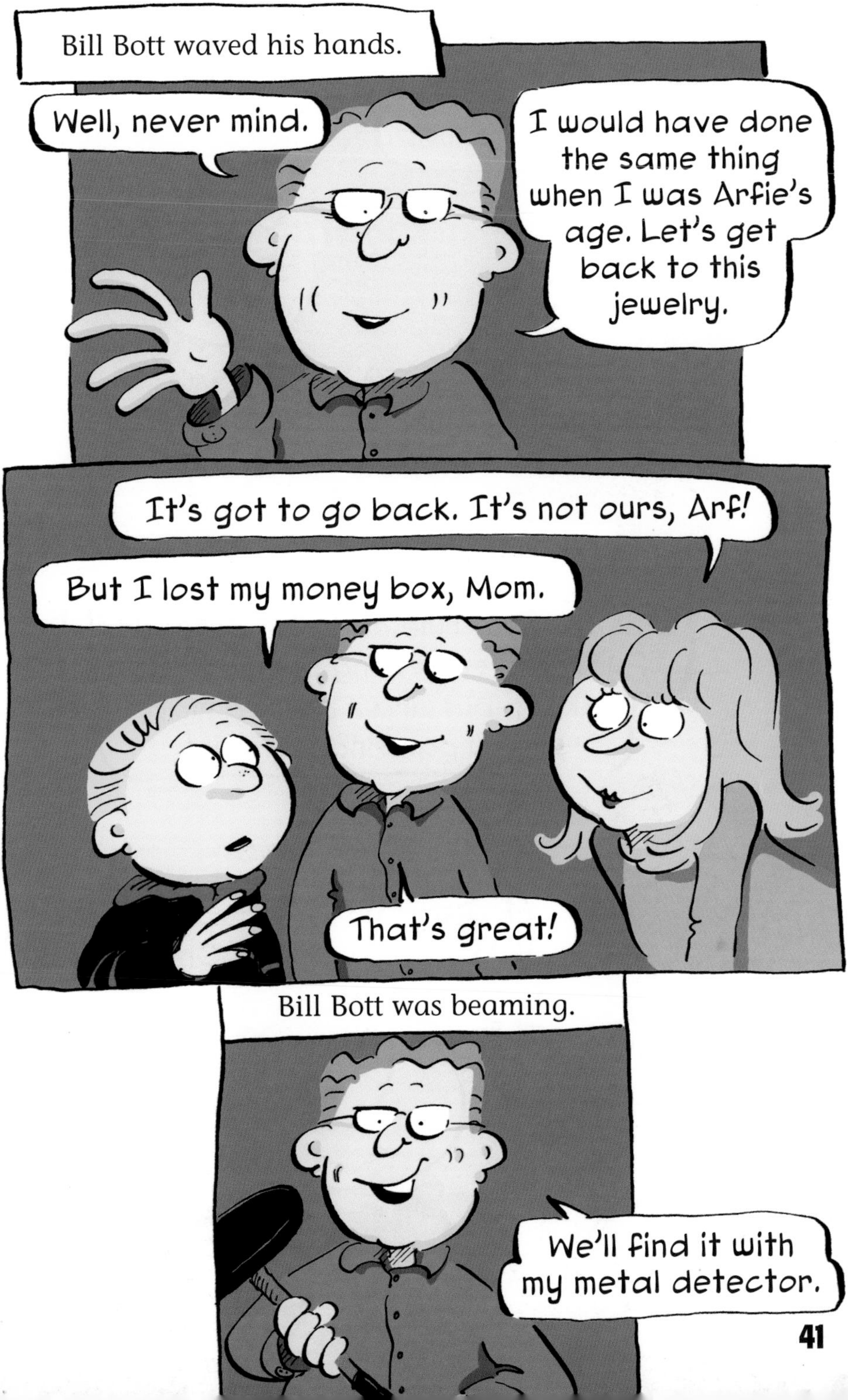

Bill Bott waved his hands.
Well, never mind.
I would have done the same thing when I was Arfie's age. Let's get back to this jewelry.
It's got to go back. It's not ours, Arf!
But I lost my money box, Mom.
That's great!
Bill Bott was beaming.
We'll find it with my metal detector.

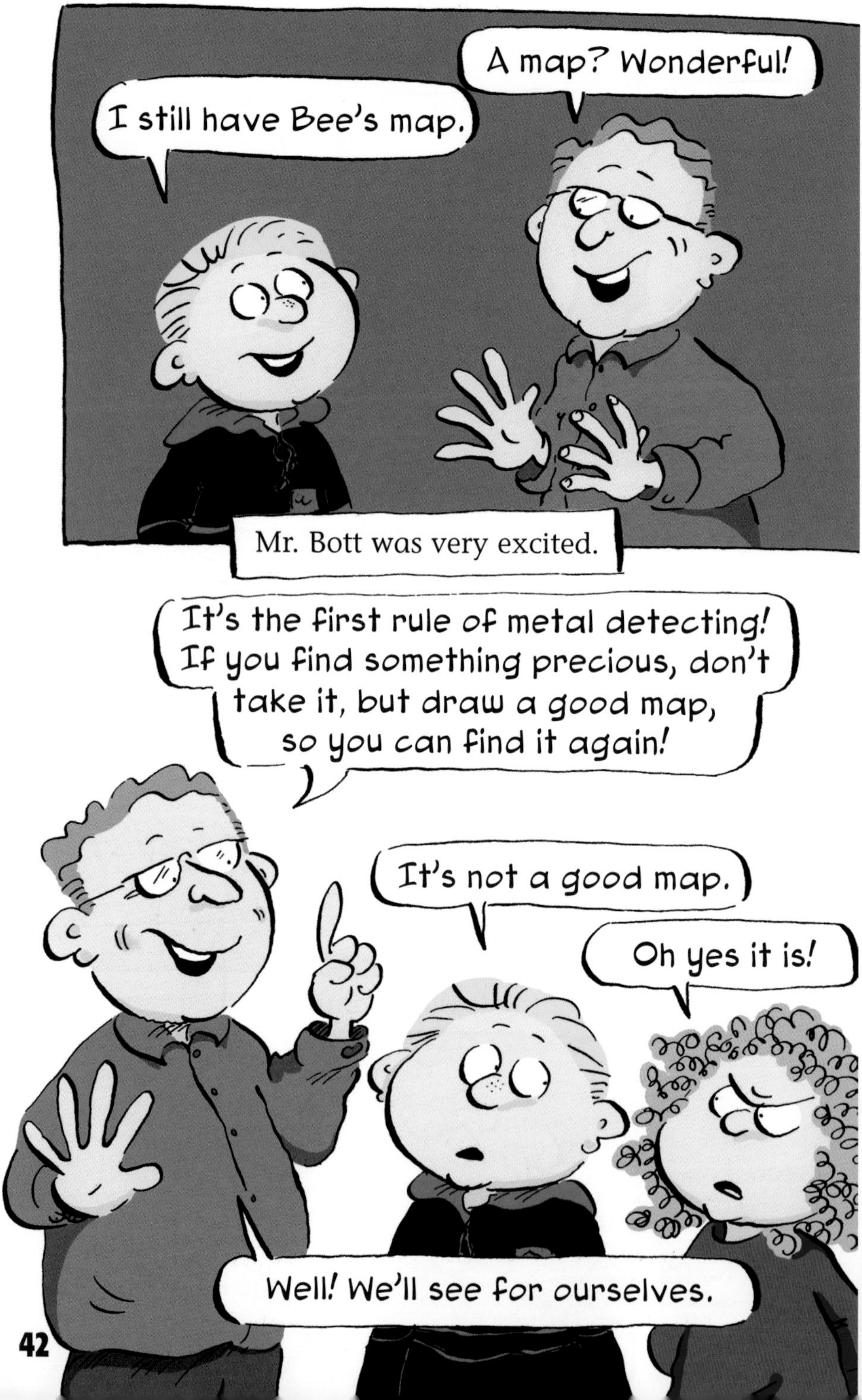
I still have Bee's map.
A map? Wonderful!
Mr. Bott was very excited.
It's the first rule of metal detecting! If you find something precious, don't take it, but draw a good map, so you can find it again!
It's not a good map.
Oh yes it is!
Well! We'll see for ourselves.

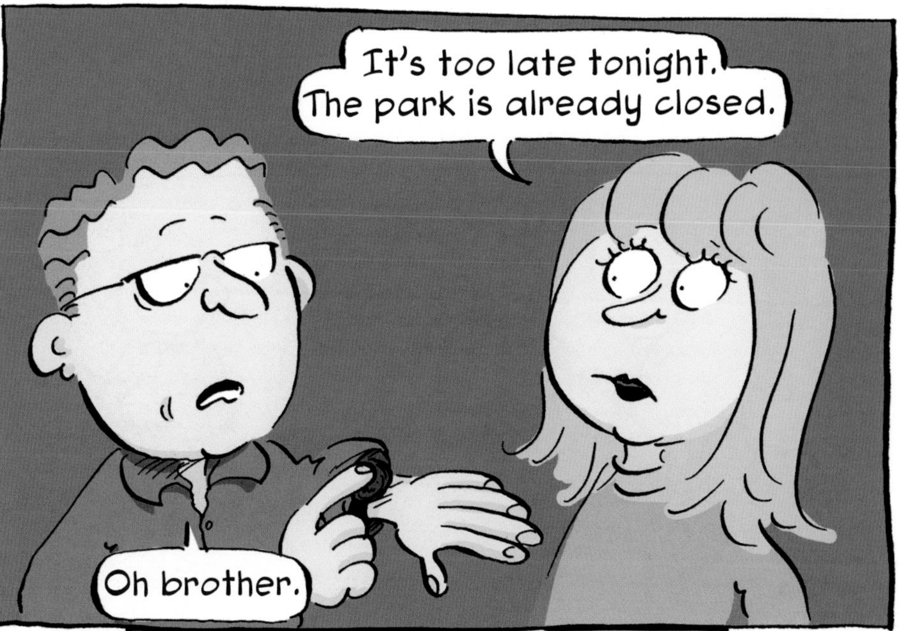
It's too late tonight. The park is already closed.
Oh brother.

Mr. Bott sighed loudly.

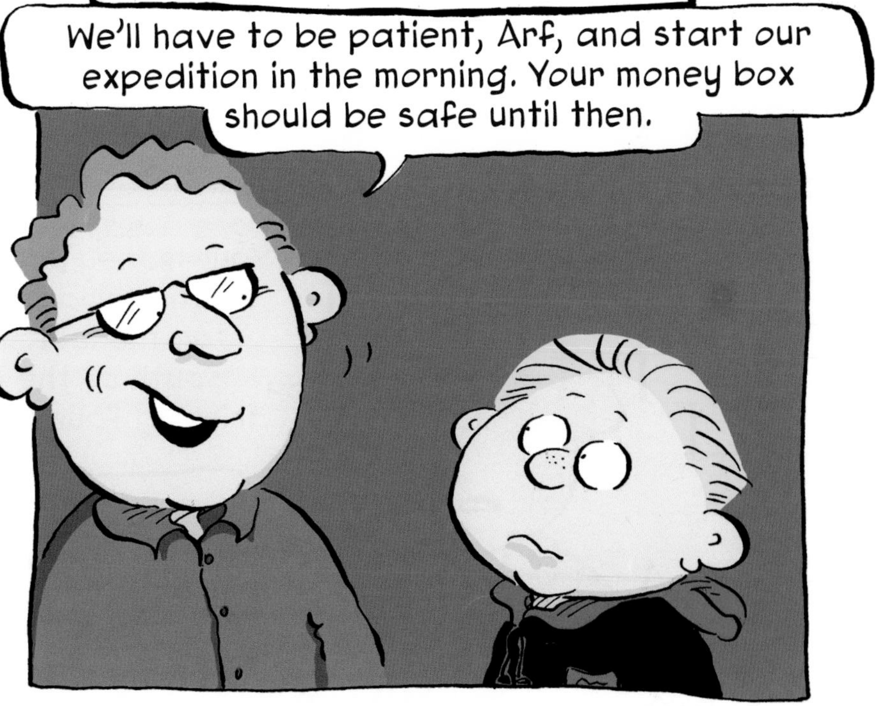
We'll have to be patient, Arf, and start our expedition in the morning. Your money box should be safe until then.

# CHAPTER FIVE

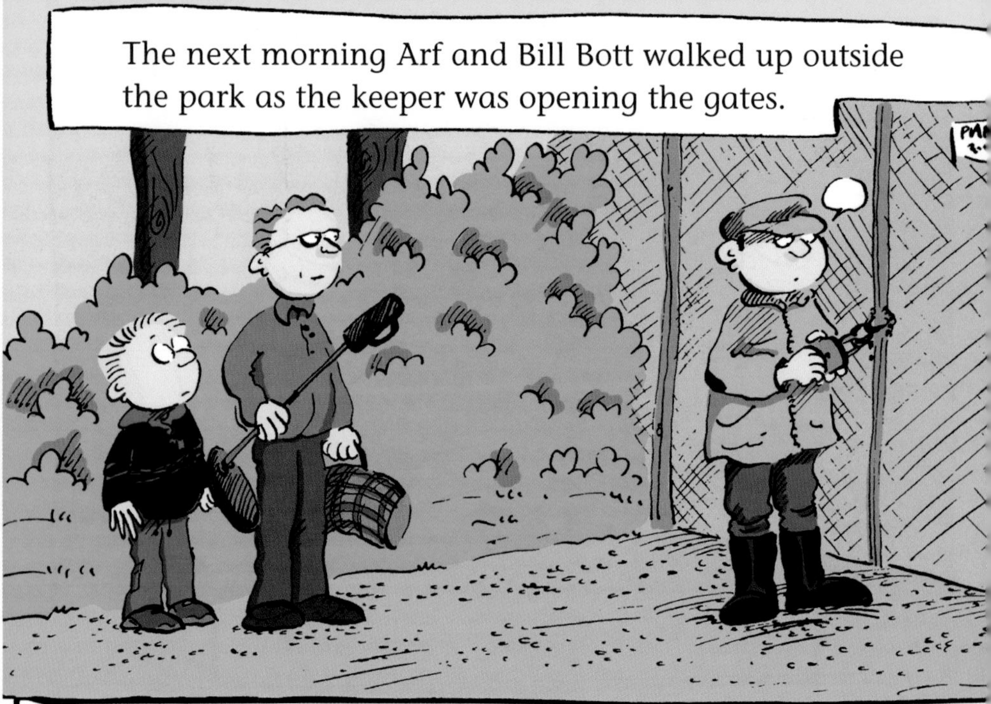
The next morning Arf and Bill Bott walked up outside the park as the keeper was opening the gates.

Arf led the way to the fountain. Then Bill put down his bag and Arf got out Bee's map.

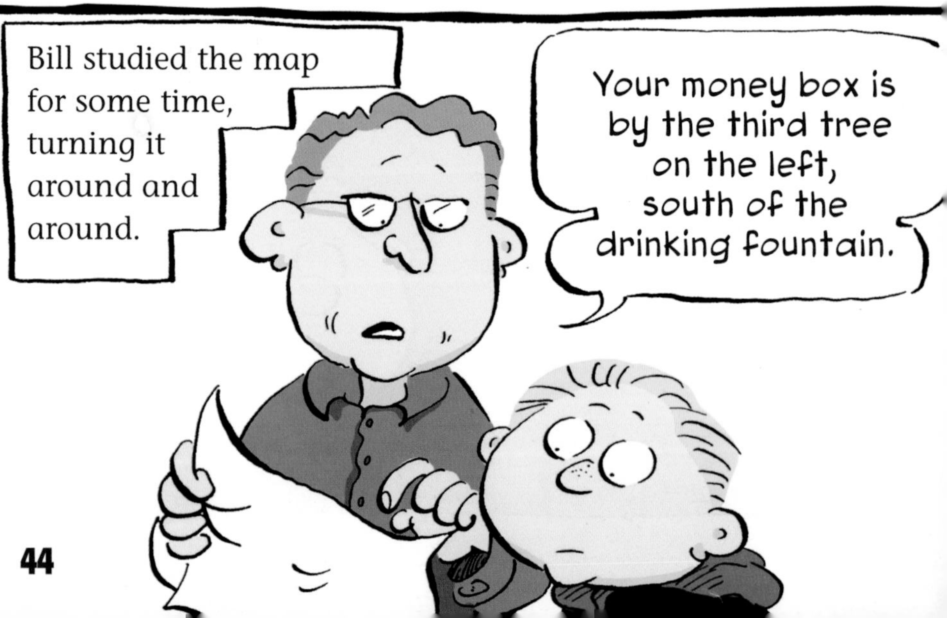
Bill studied the map for some time, turning it around and around.
Your money box is by the third tree on the left, south of the drinking fountain.

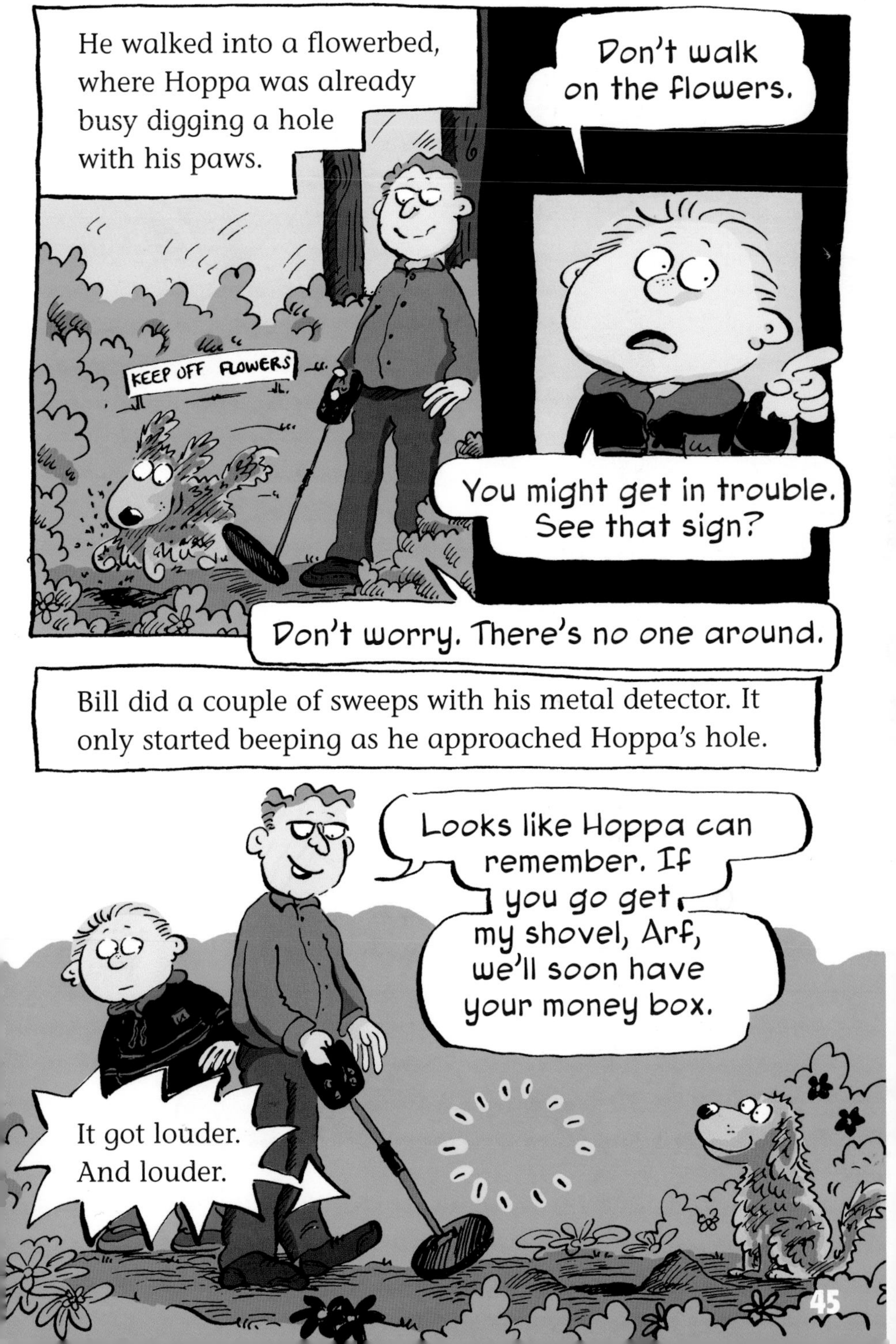
He walked into a flowerbed, where Hoppa was already busy digging a hole with his paws.
Don't walk on the flowers.
KEEP OFF FLOWERS
You might get in trouble. See that sign?
Don't worry. There's no one around.
Bill did a couple of sweeps with his metal detector. It only started beeping as he approached Hoppa's hole.
Looks like Hoppa can remember. If you go get my shovel, Arf, we'll soon have your money box.
It got louder. And louder.

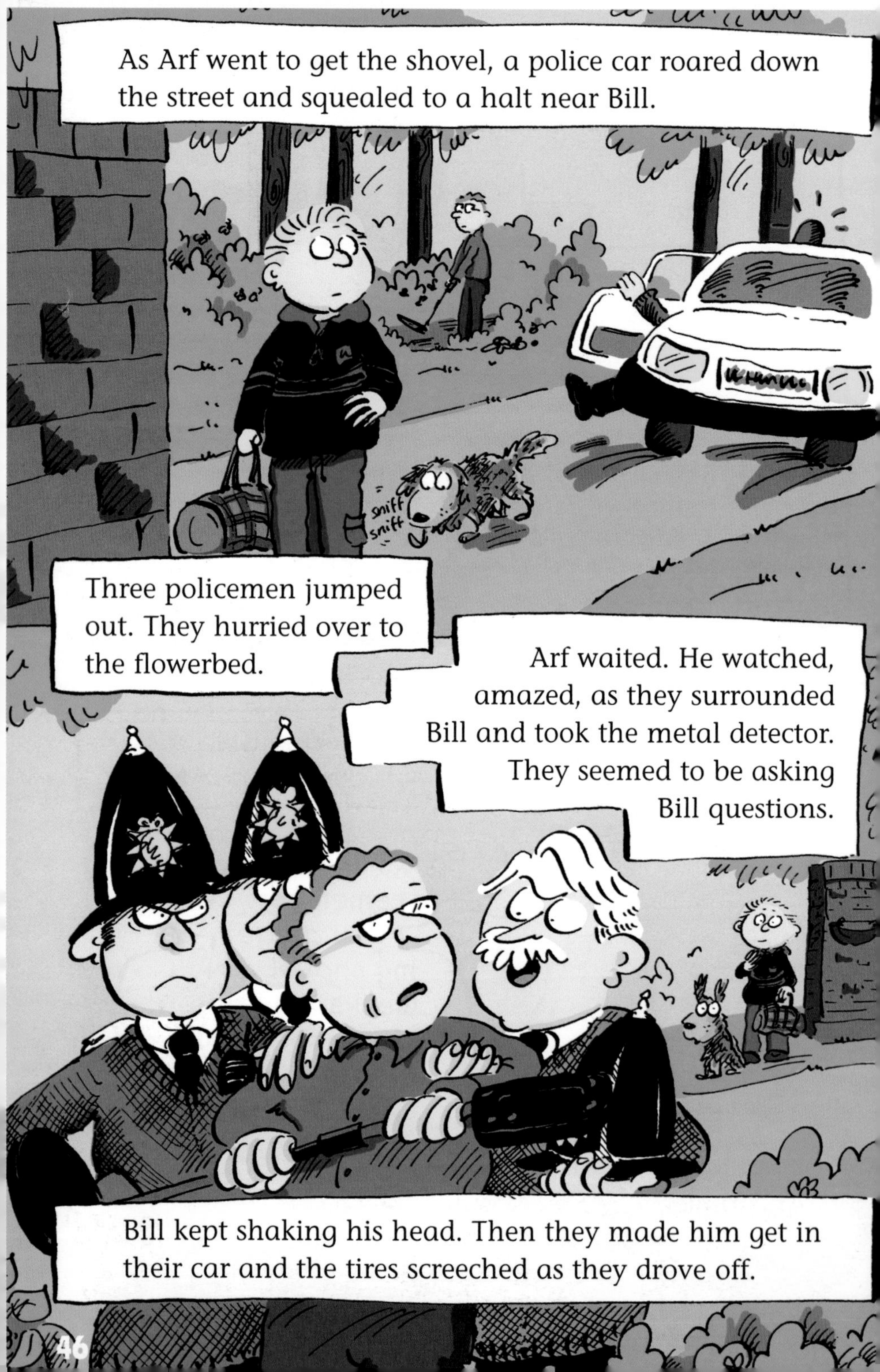
As Arf went to get the shovel, a police car roared down the street and squealed to a halt near Bill.
sniff sniff
Three policemen jumped out. They hurried over to the flowerbed.
Arf waited. He watched, amazed, as they surrounded Bill and took the metal detector. They seemed to be asking Bill questions.
Bill kept shaking his head. Then they made him get in their car and the tires screeched as they drove off.

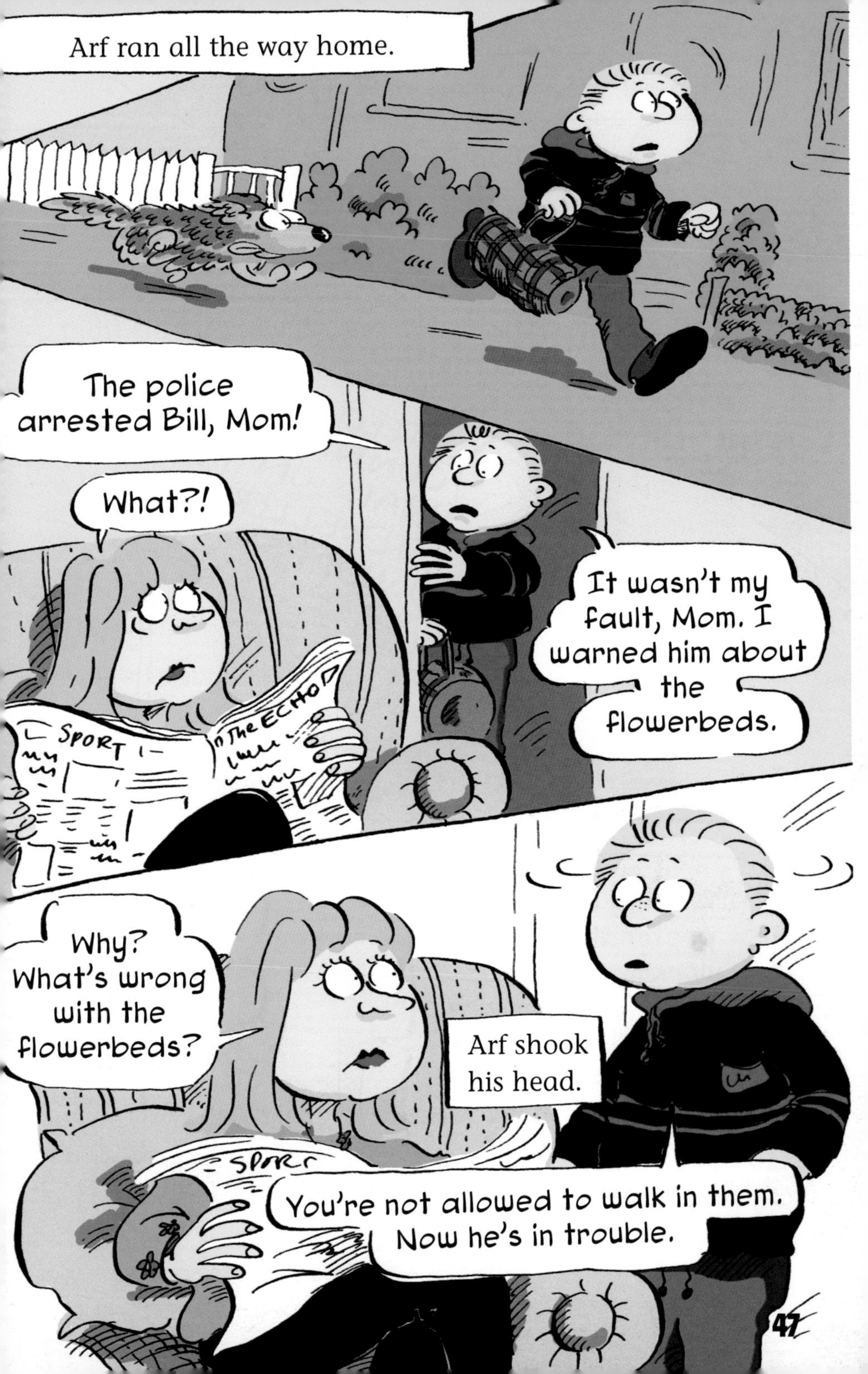
Arf ran all the way home.
The police arrested Bill, Mom!
What?!
It wasn't my fault, Mom. I warned him about the flowerbeds.
Why? What's wrong with the flowerbeds?
Arf shook his head.
You're not allowed to walk in them. Now he's in trouble.
SPORT
The ECHO

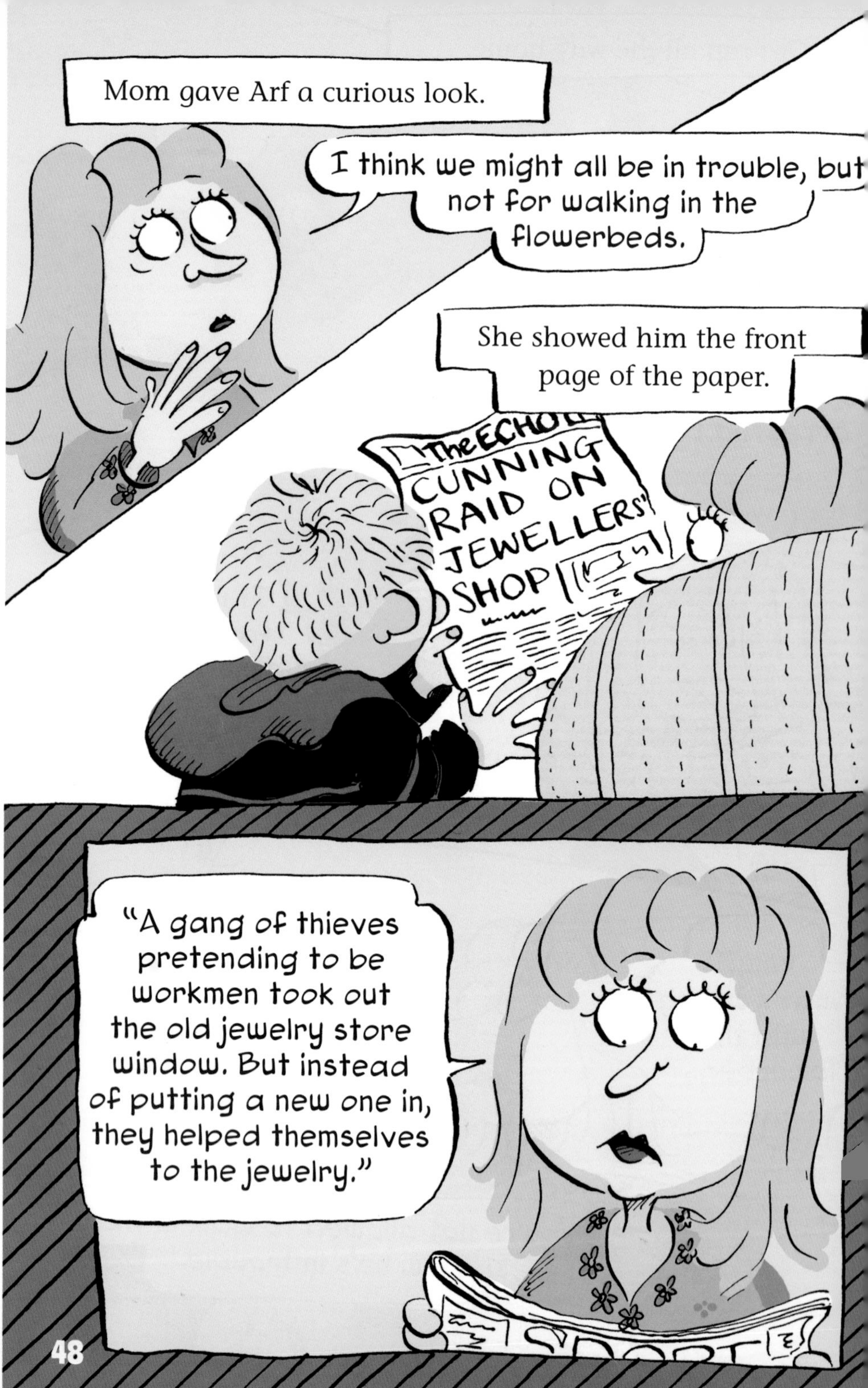
Mom gave Arf a curious look.
I think we might all be in trouble, but not for walking in the flowerbeds.
She showed him the front page of the paper.
The ECHO
CUNNING RAID ON JEWELLERS' SHOP
"A gang of thieves pretending to be workmen took out the old jewelry store window. But instead of putting a new one in, they helped themselves to the jewelry."

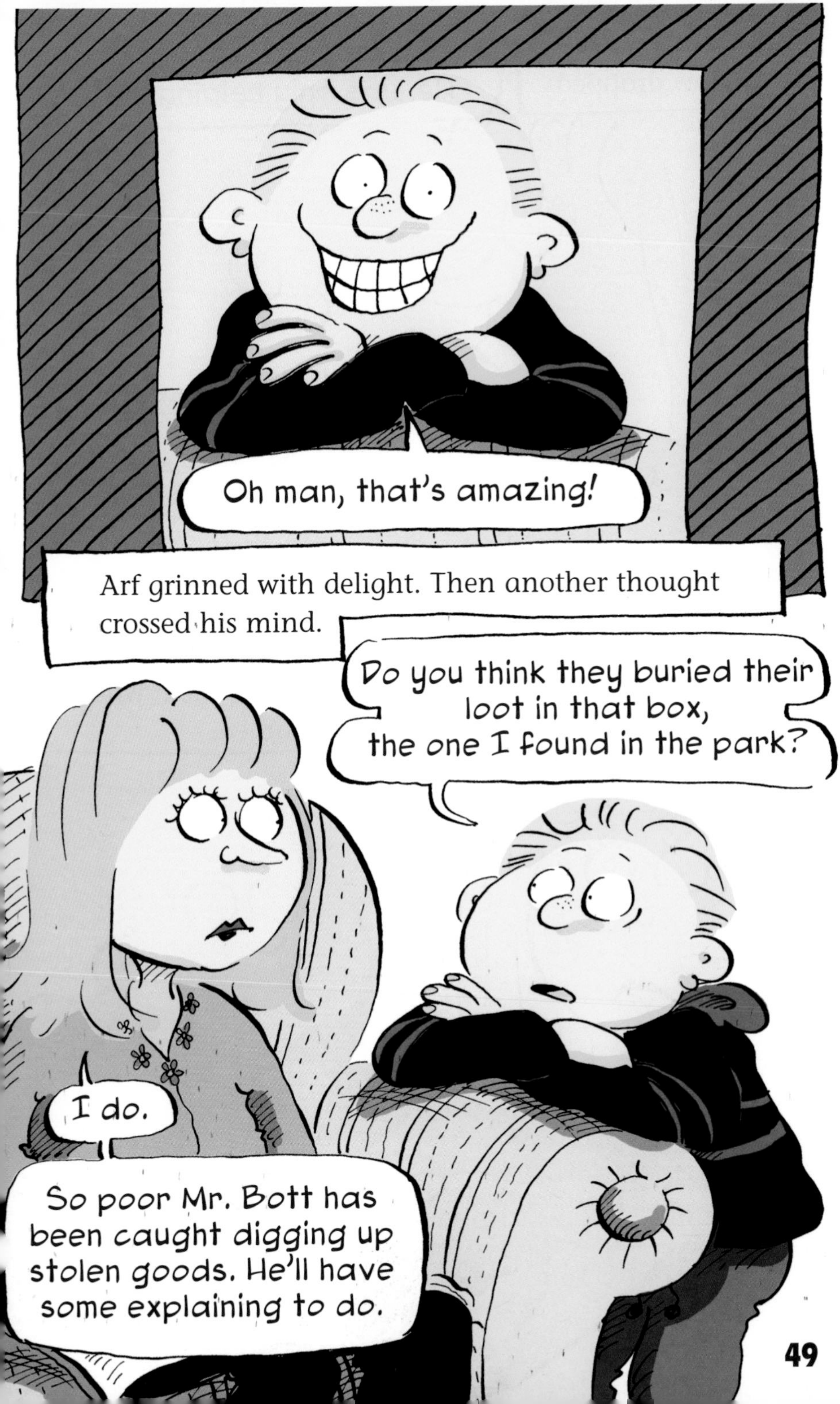
Oh man, that's amazing!
Arf grinned with delight. Then another thought crossed his mind.
Do you think they buried their loot in that box, the one I found in the park?
I do.
So poor Mr. Bott has been caught digging up stolen goods. He'll have some explaining to do.

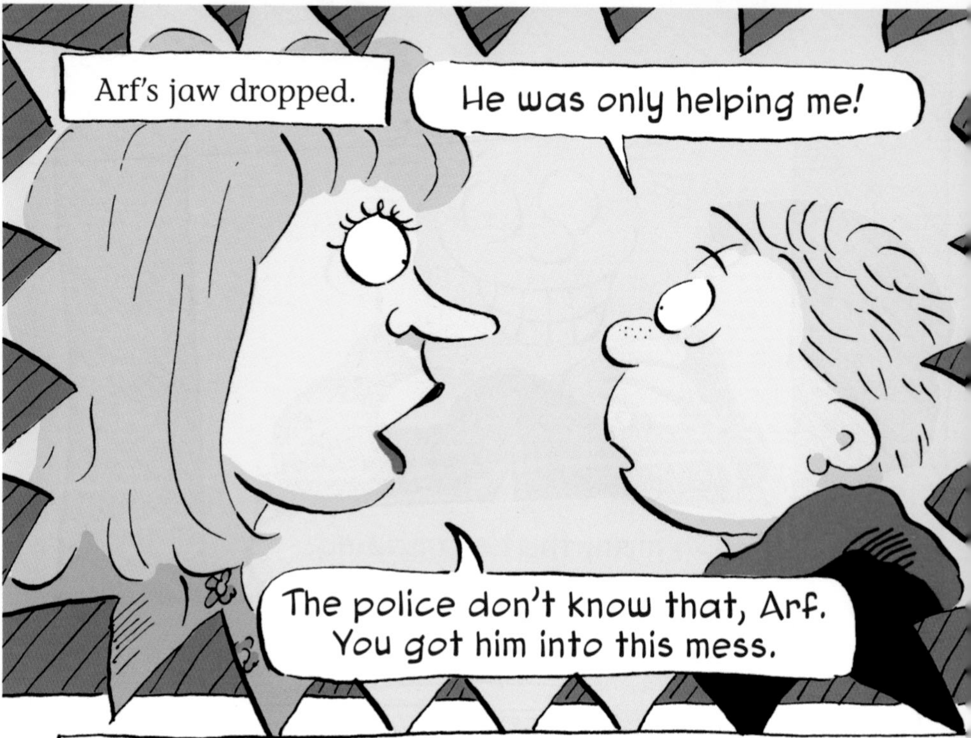
Arf's jaw dropped.
He was only helping me!
The police don't know that, Arf. You got him into this mess.

Before Mom could call the police and tell them what Arf had been up to, the front doorbell chimed.

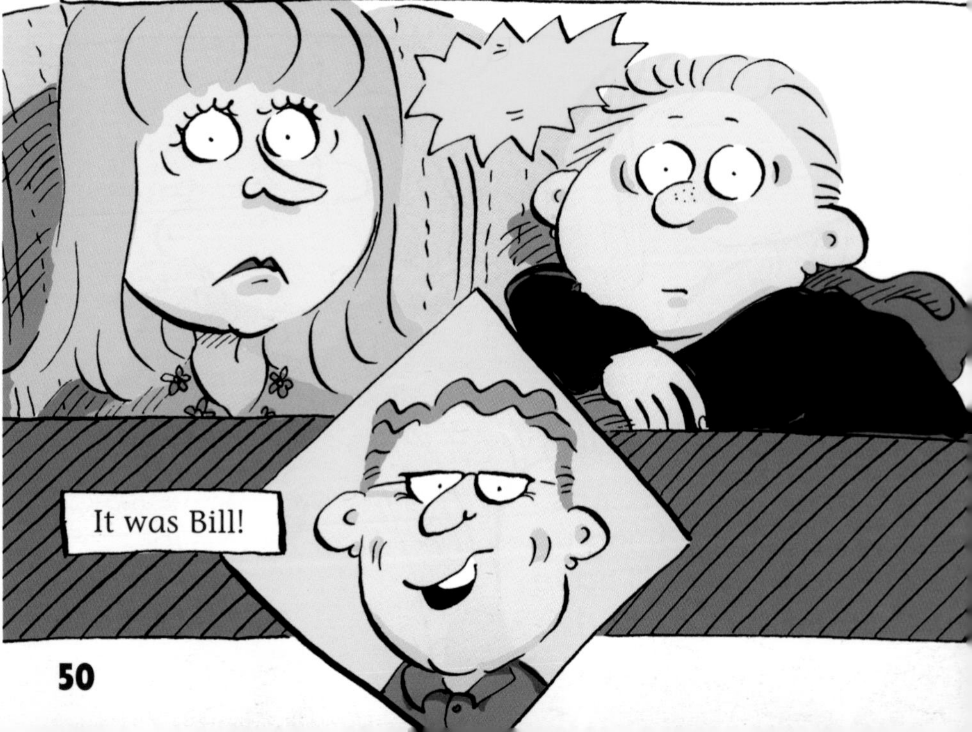
It was Bill!

# CHAPTER SIX

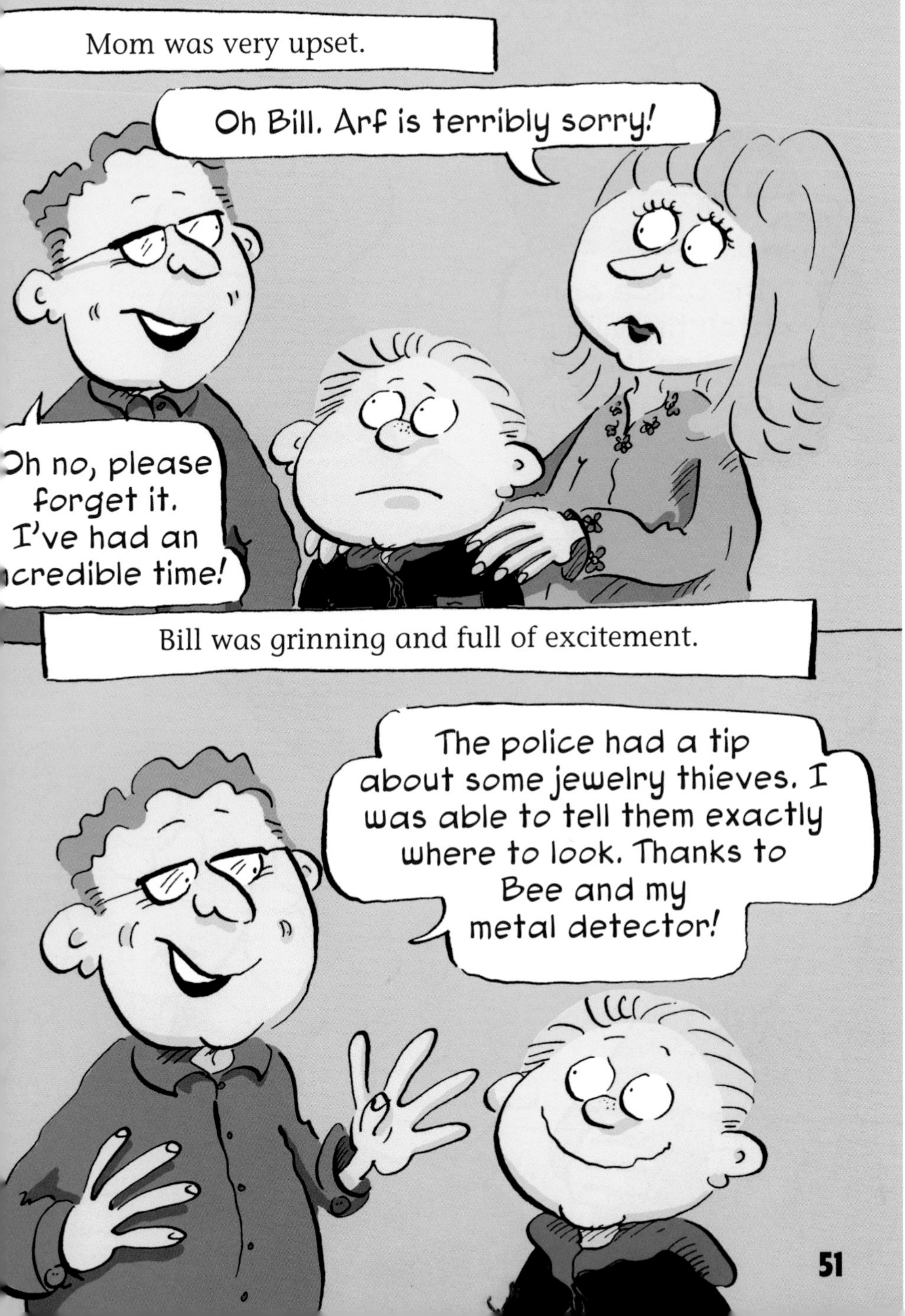
Mom was very upset.
Oh Bill. Arf is terribly sorry!
Oh no, please forget it. I've had an ncredible time!
Bill was grinning and full of excitement.
The police had a tip about some jewelry thieves. I was able to tell them exactly where to look. Thanks to Bee and my metal detector!

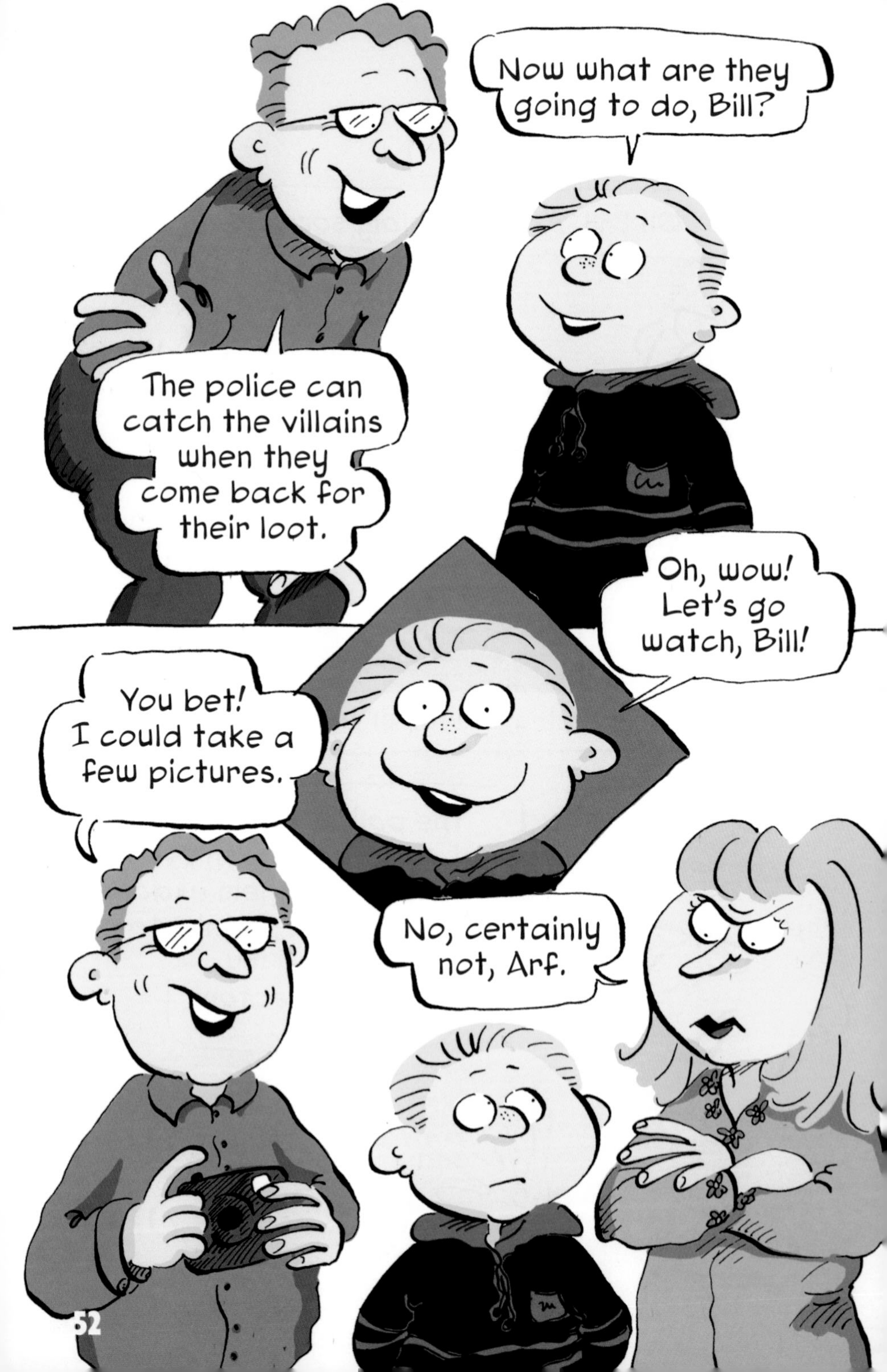
Now what are they going to do, Bill?
The police can catch the villains when they come back for their loot.
Oh, wow! Let's go watch, Bill!
You bet! I could take a few pictures.
No, certainly not, Arf.

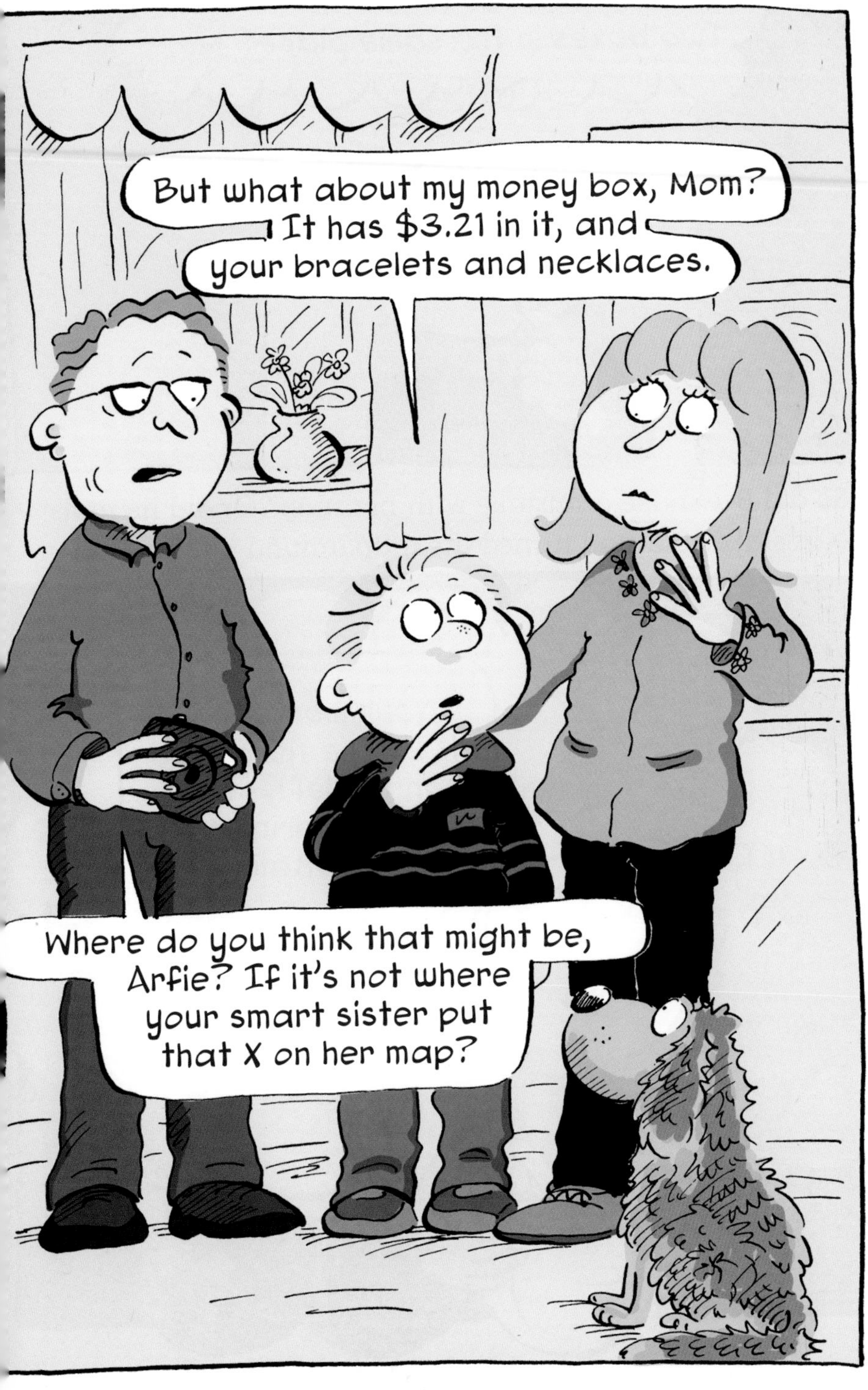
But what about my money box, Mom? It has $3.21 in it, and your bracelets and necklaces.
Where do you think that might be, Arfie? If it's not where your smart sister put that X on her map?

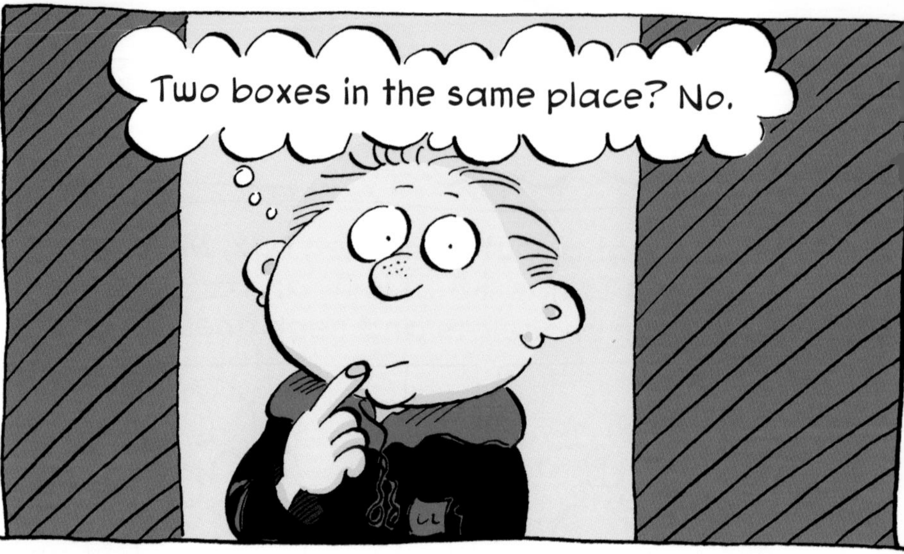
Two boxes in the same place? No.

So did Bee make a mistake with her map? Or did he make a mistake? Bill had turned the map around and around.

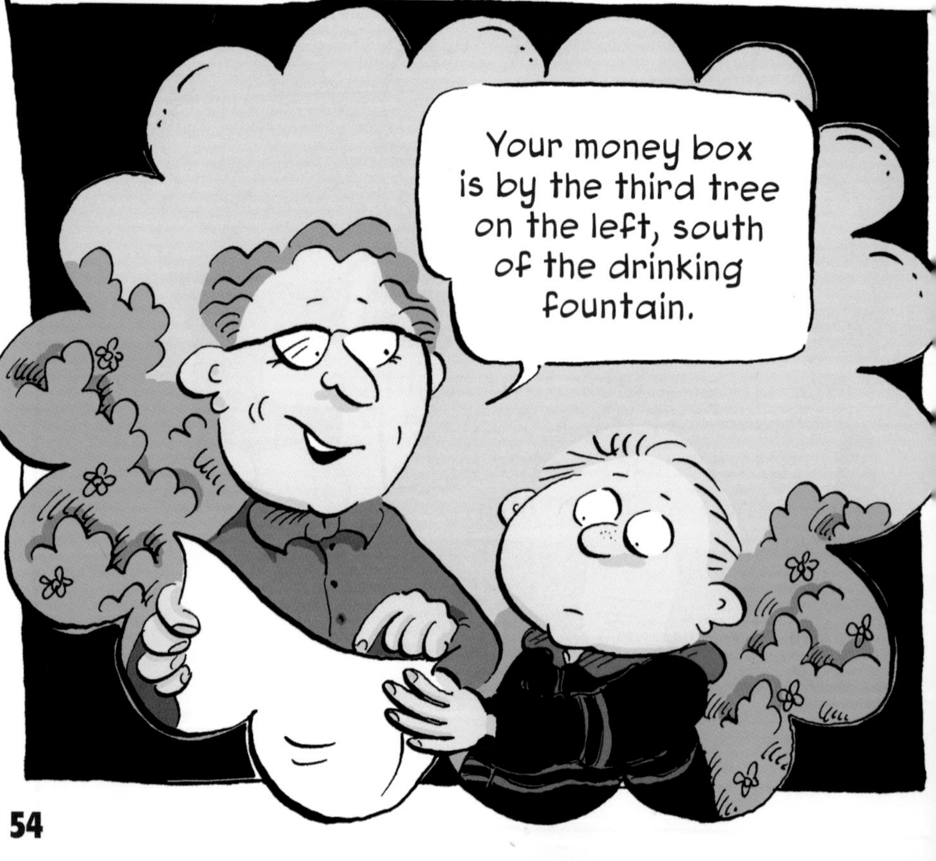
Your money box is by the third tree on the left, south of the drinking fountain.

Arf hadn't checked that the first time, thanks to Gloria breathing down his neck! What if he read the map upside down?

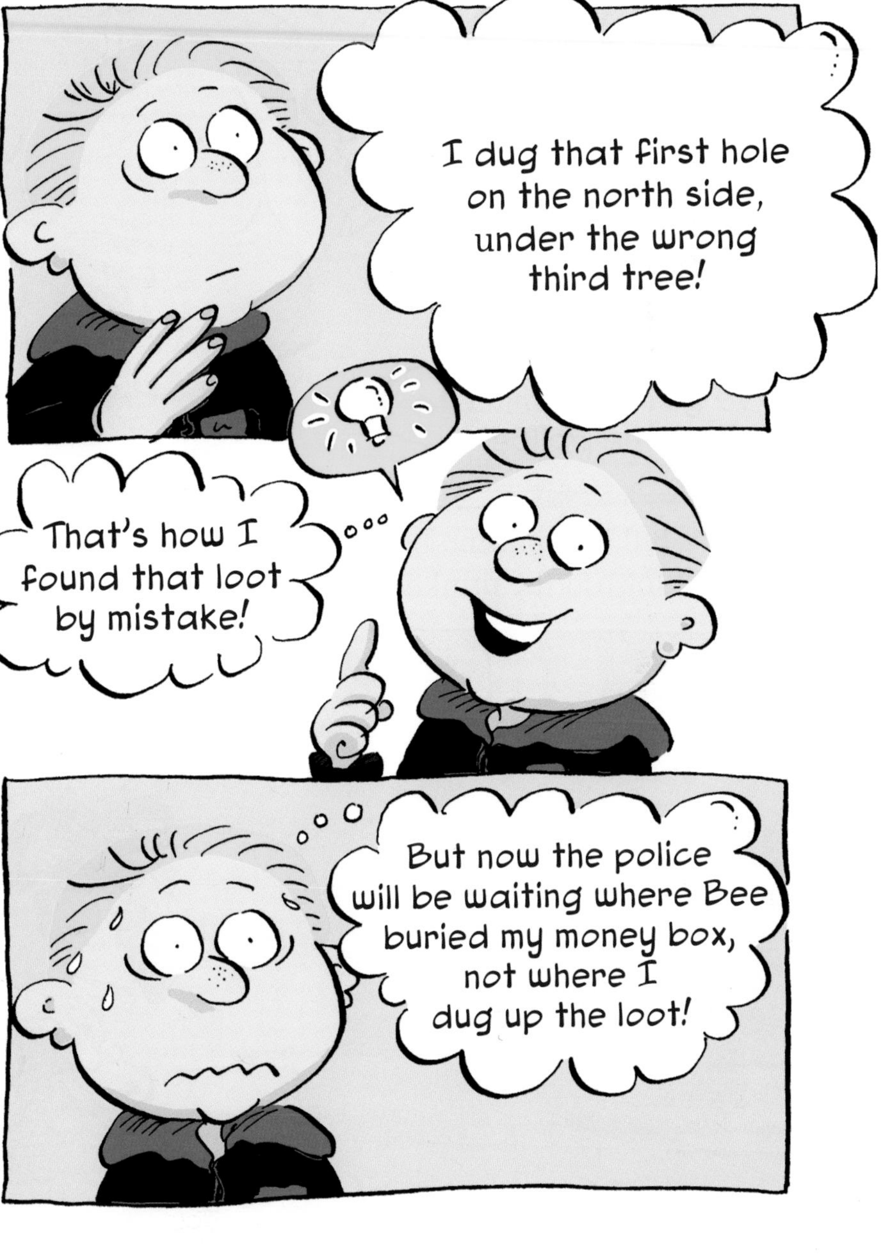
I dug that first hole on the north side, under the wrong third tree!
That's how I found that loot by mistake!
But now the police will be waiting where Bee buried my money box, not where I dug up the loot!

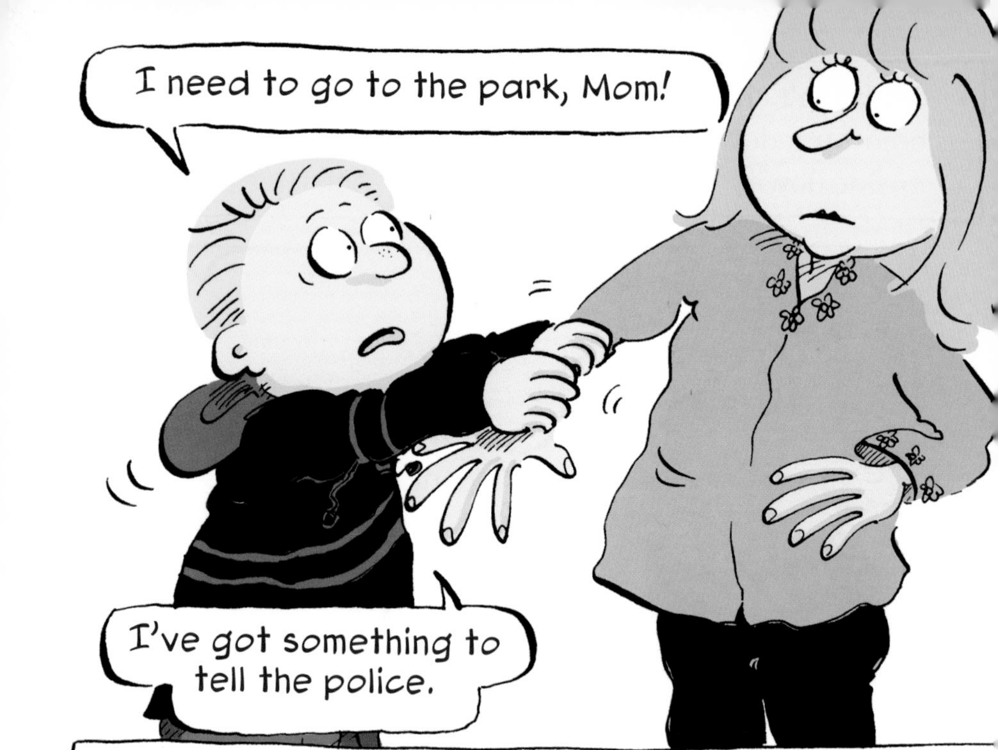
I need to go to the park, Mom!
I've got something to tell the police.

With Bill Bott puffing behind him, Arf ran down the street toward the drinking fountain.

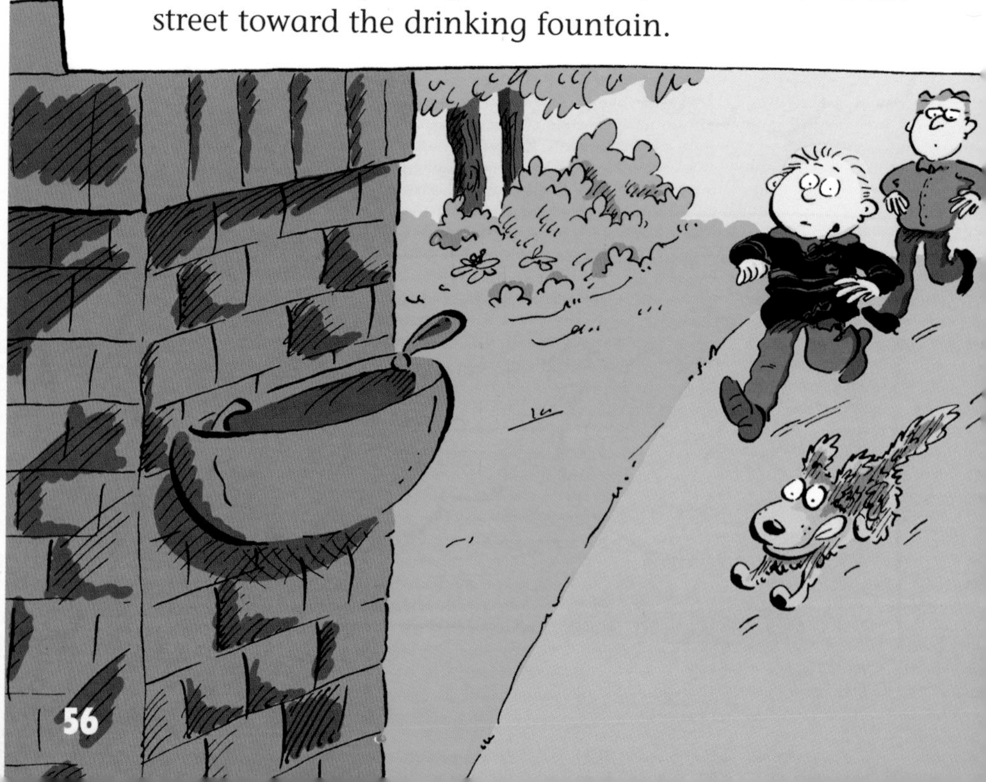

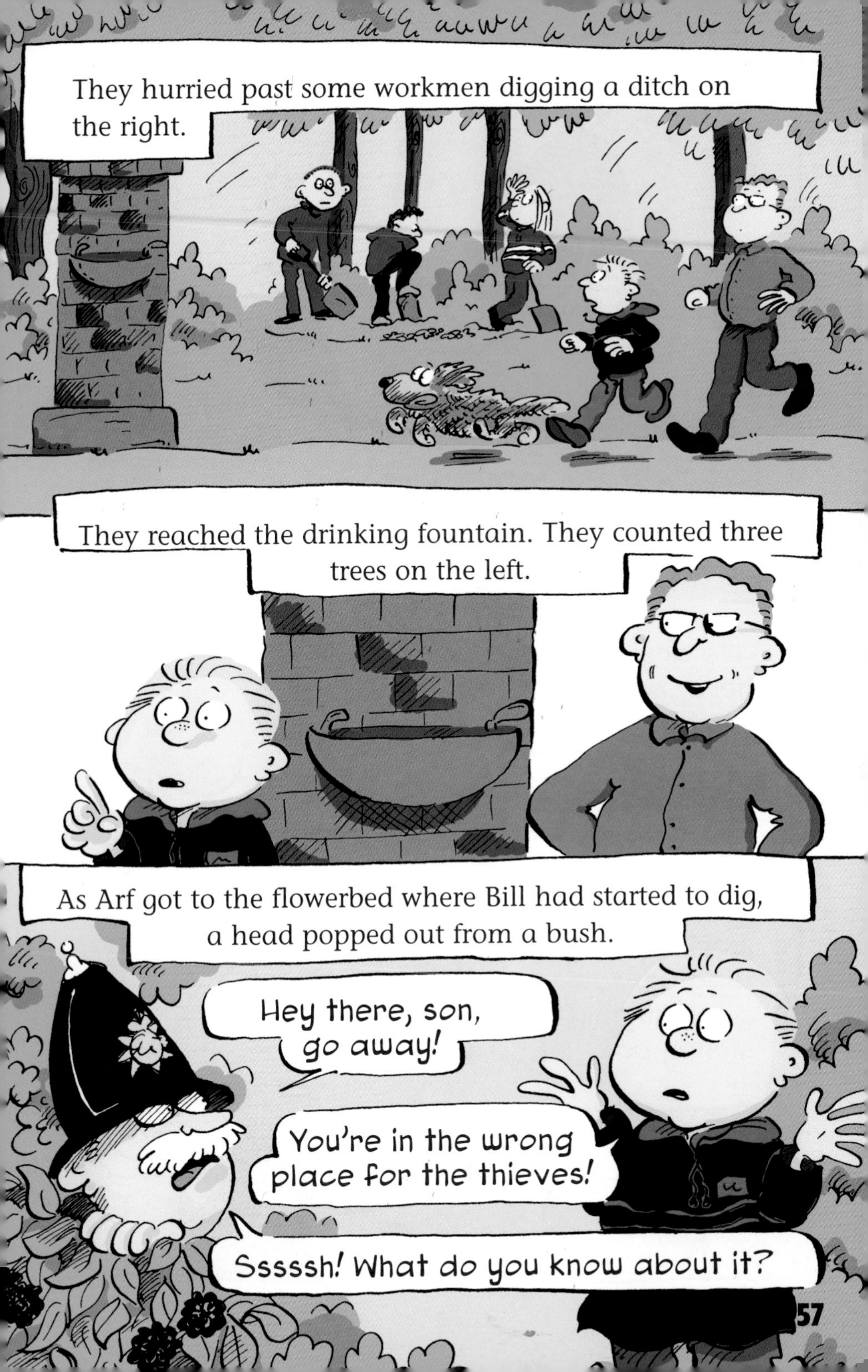
They hurried past some workmen digging a ditch on the right.
They reached the drinking fountain. They counted three trees on the left.
As Arf got to the flowerbed where Bill had started to dig, a head popped out from a bush.
Hey there, son, go away!
You're in the wrong place for the thieves!
Ssssh! What do you know about it?

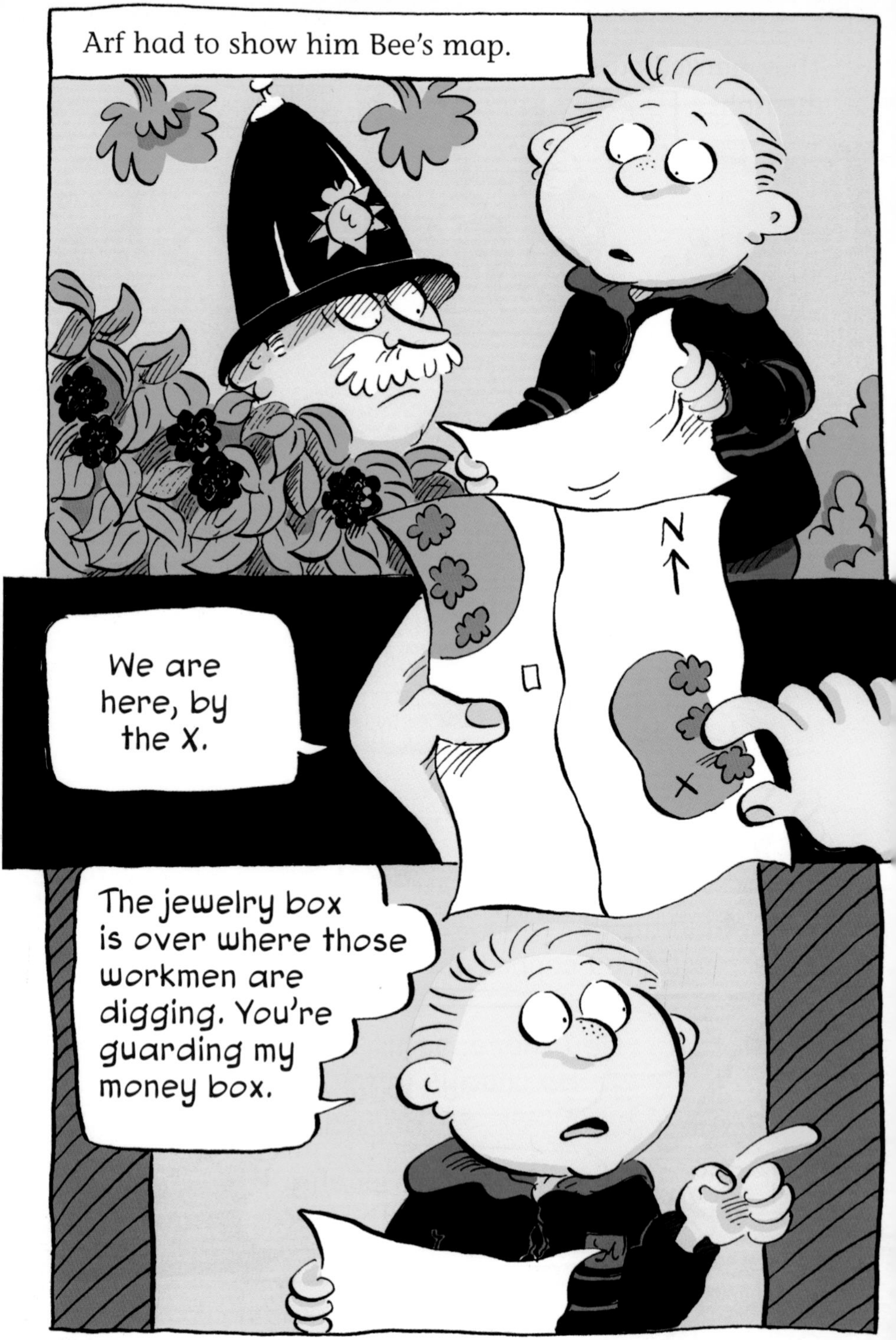
Arf had to show him Bee's map.
N
We are here, by the X.
The jewelry box is over where those workmen are digging. You're guarding my money box.

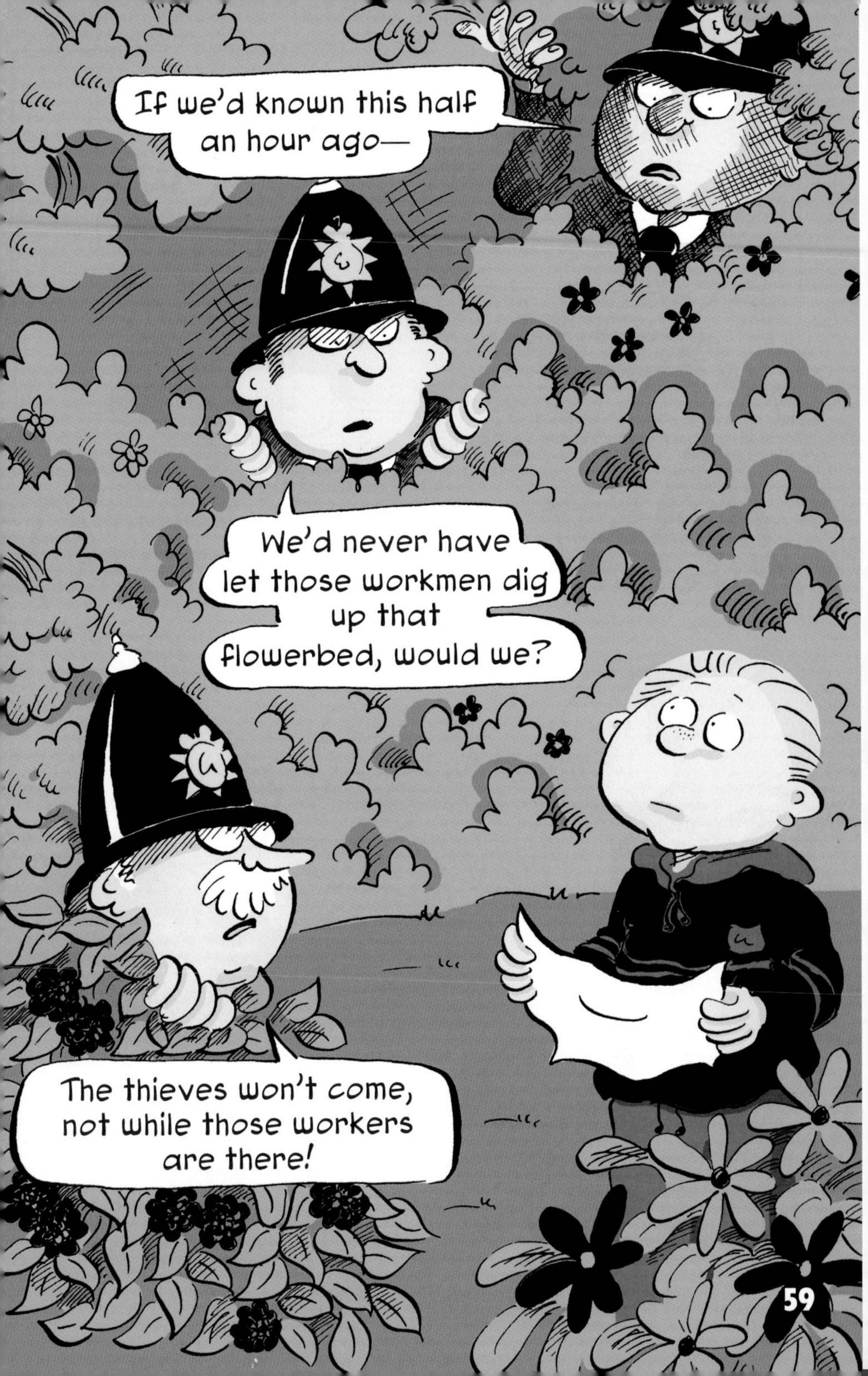

If we'd known this half an hour ago—
We'd never have let those workmen dig up that flowerbed, would we?
The thieves won't come, not while those workers are there!

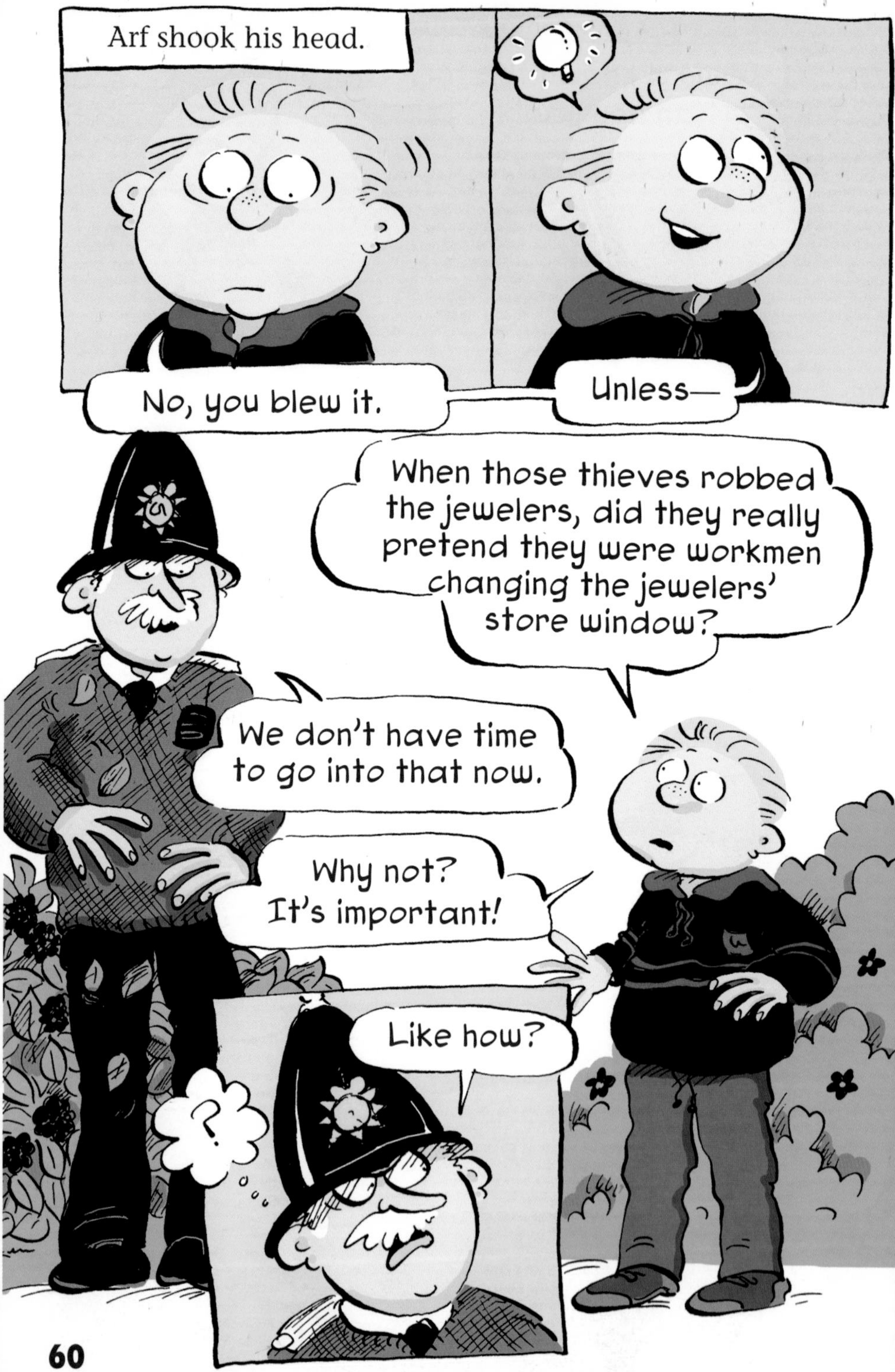
Arf shook his head.
No, you blew it.
Unless—
When those thieves robbed the jewelers, did they really pretend they were workmen changing the jewelers' store window?
We don't have time to go into that now.
Why not? It's important!
Like how?
?

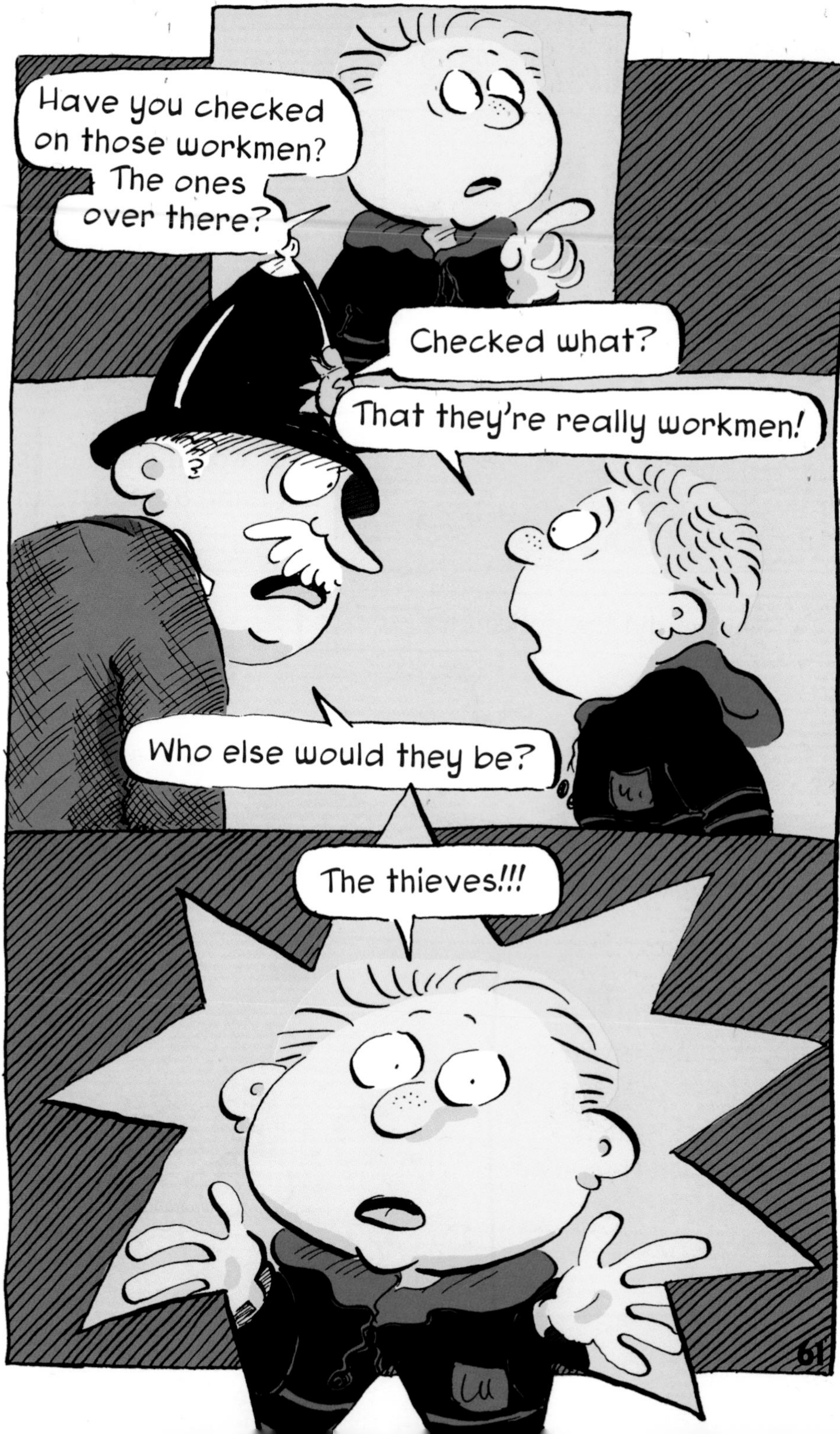
Have you checked on those workmen? The ones over there?
Checked what?
That they're really workmen!
Who else would they be?
The thieves!!!

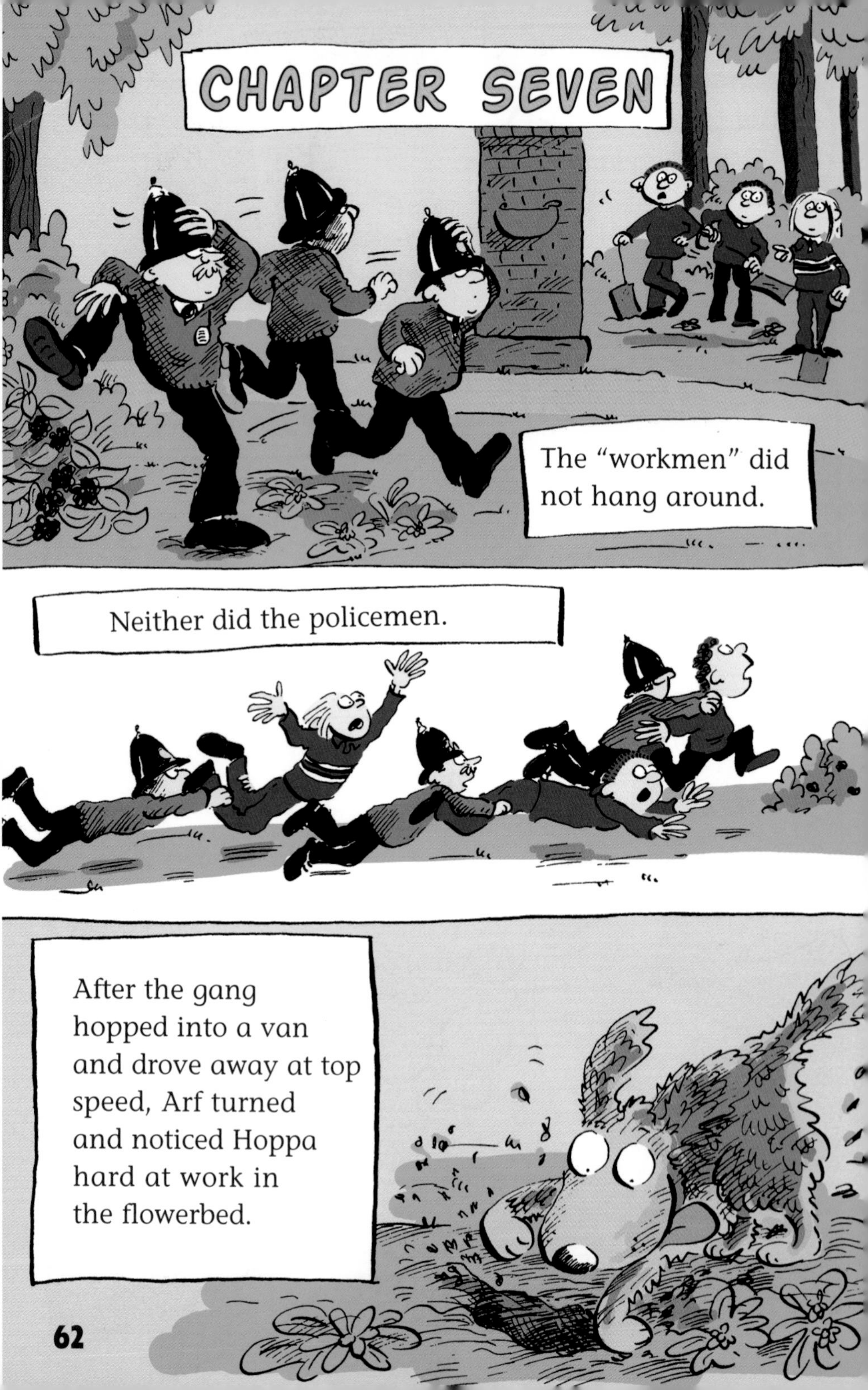
CHAPTER SEVEN
The "workmen" did not hang around.
Neither did the policemen.
After the gang hopped into a van and drove away at top speed, Arf turned and noticed Hoppa hard at work in the flowerbed.

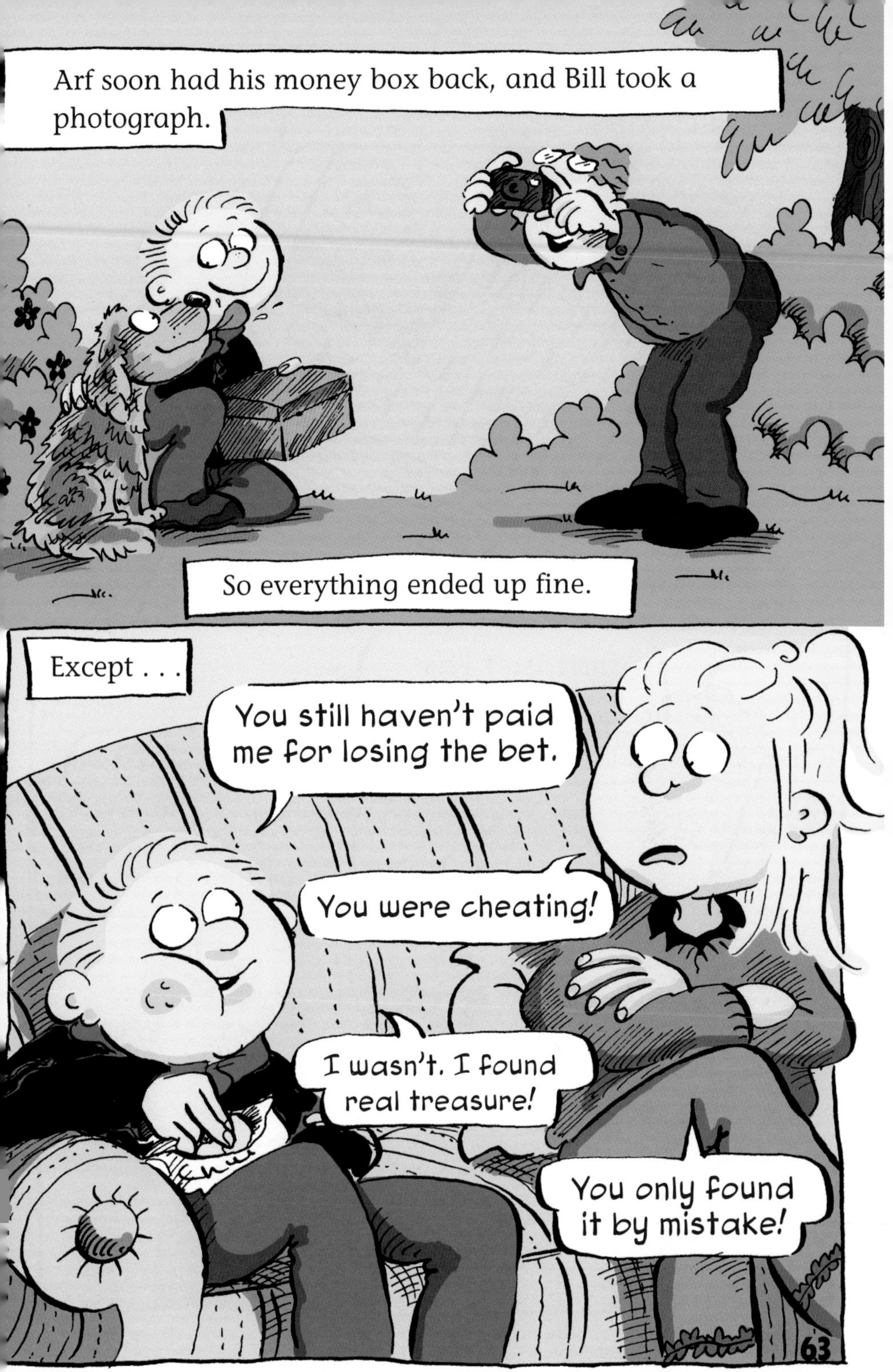

Arf soon had his money box back, and Bill took a photograph.
So everything ended up fine.
Except . . .
You still haven't paid me for losing the bet.
You were cheating!
I wasn't. I found real treasure!
You only found it by mistake!

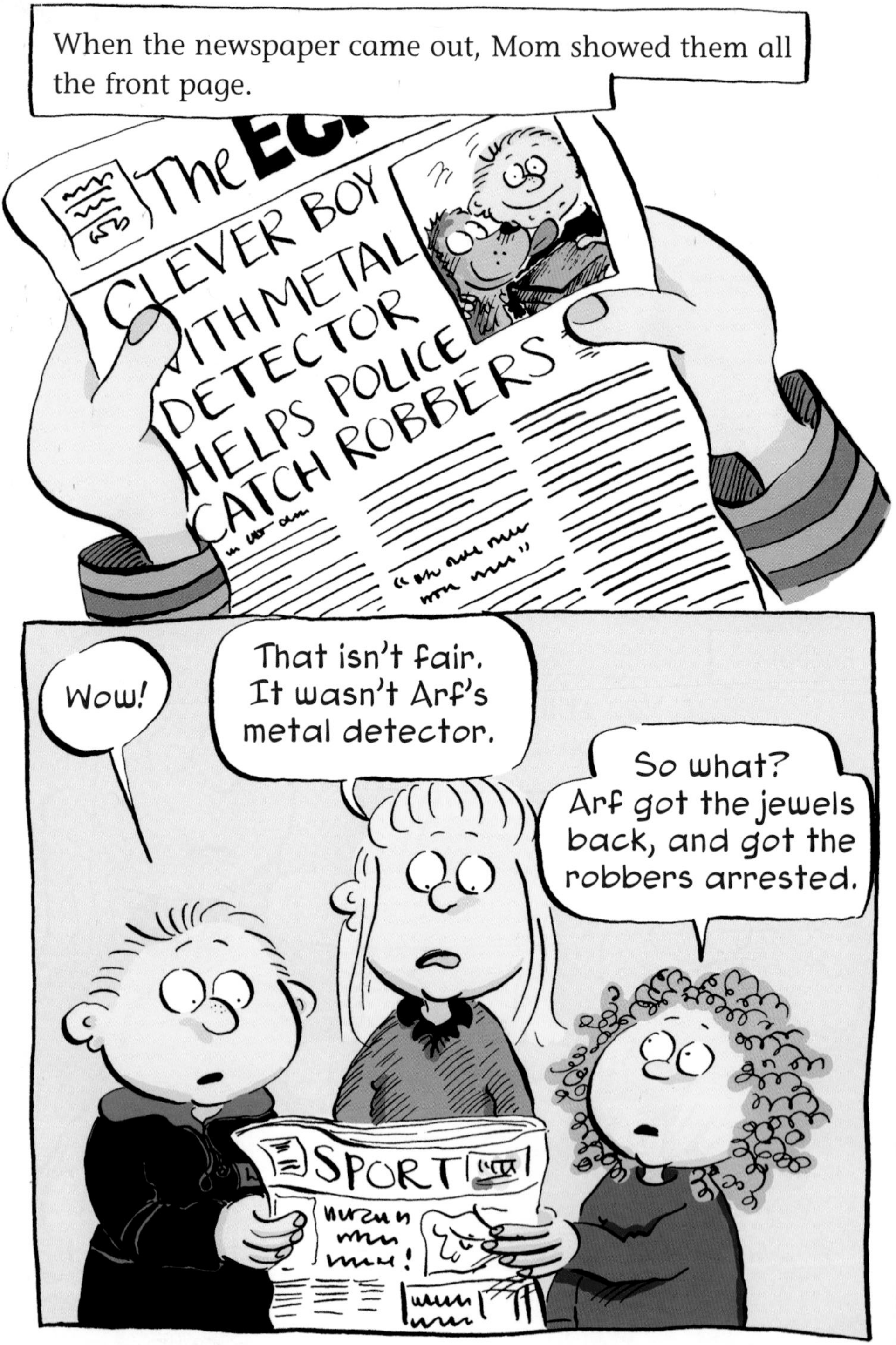
When the newspaper came out, Mom showed them all the front page.
CLEVER BOY WITH METAL DETECTOR HELPS POLICE CATCH ROBBERS
Wow!
That isn't fair. It wasn't Arf's metal detector.
So what? Arf got the jewels back, and got the robbers arrested.
SPORT

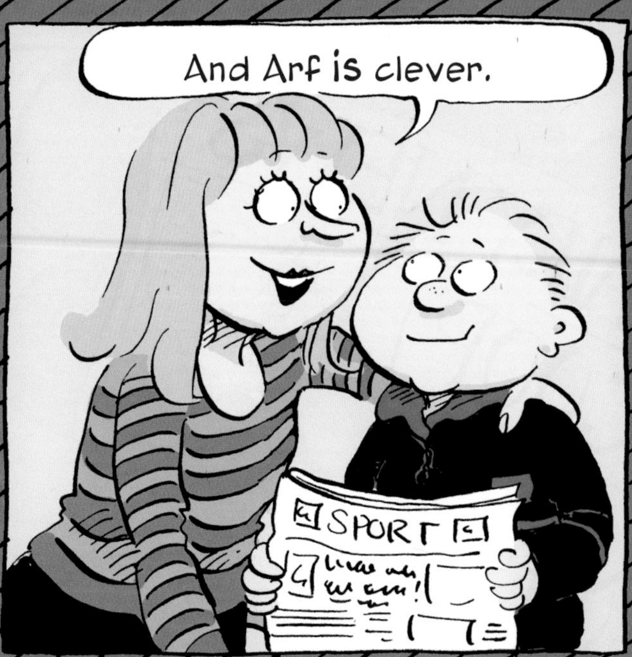
And Arf is clever.
SPORT

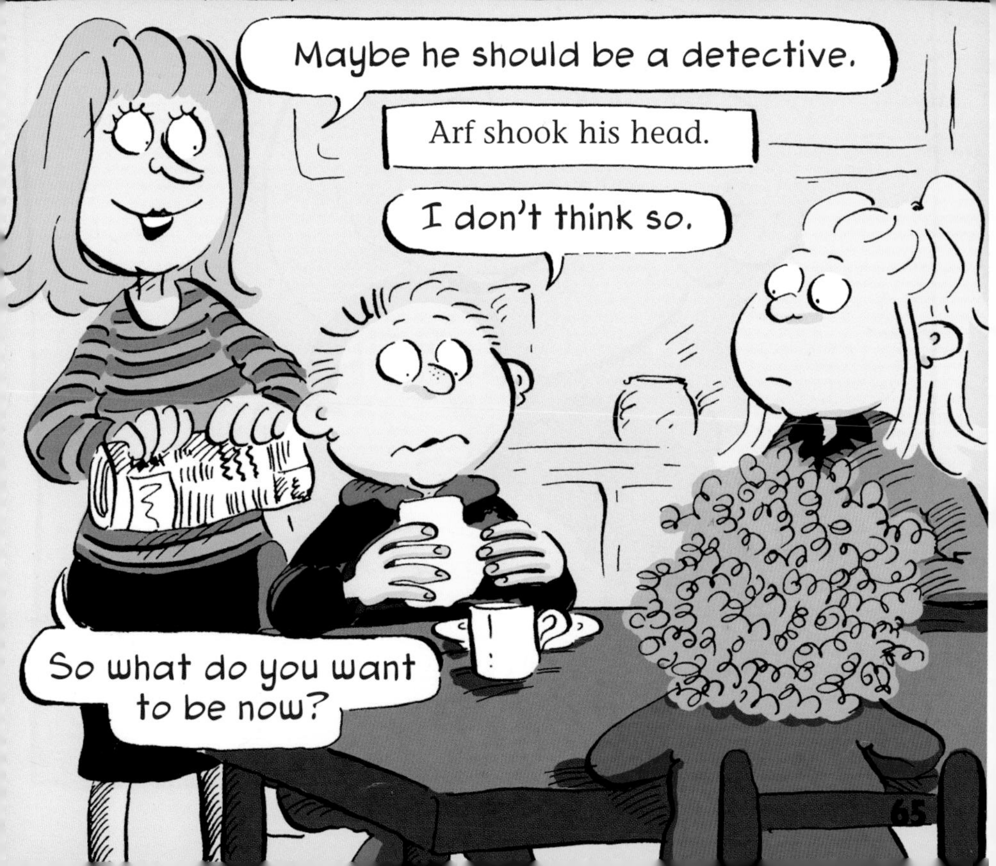
Maybe he should be a detective.
Arf shook his head.
I don't think so.
So what do you want to be now?

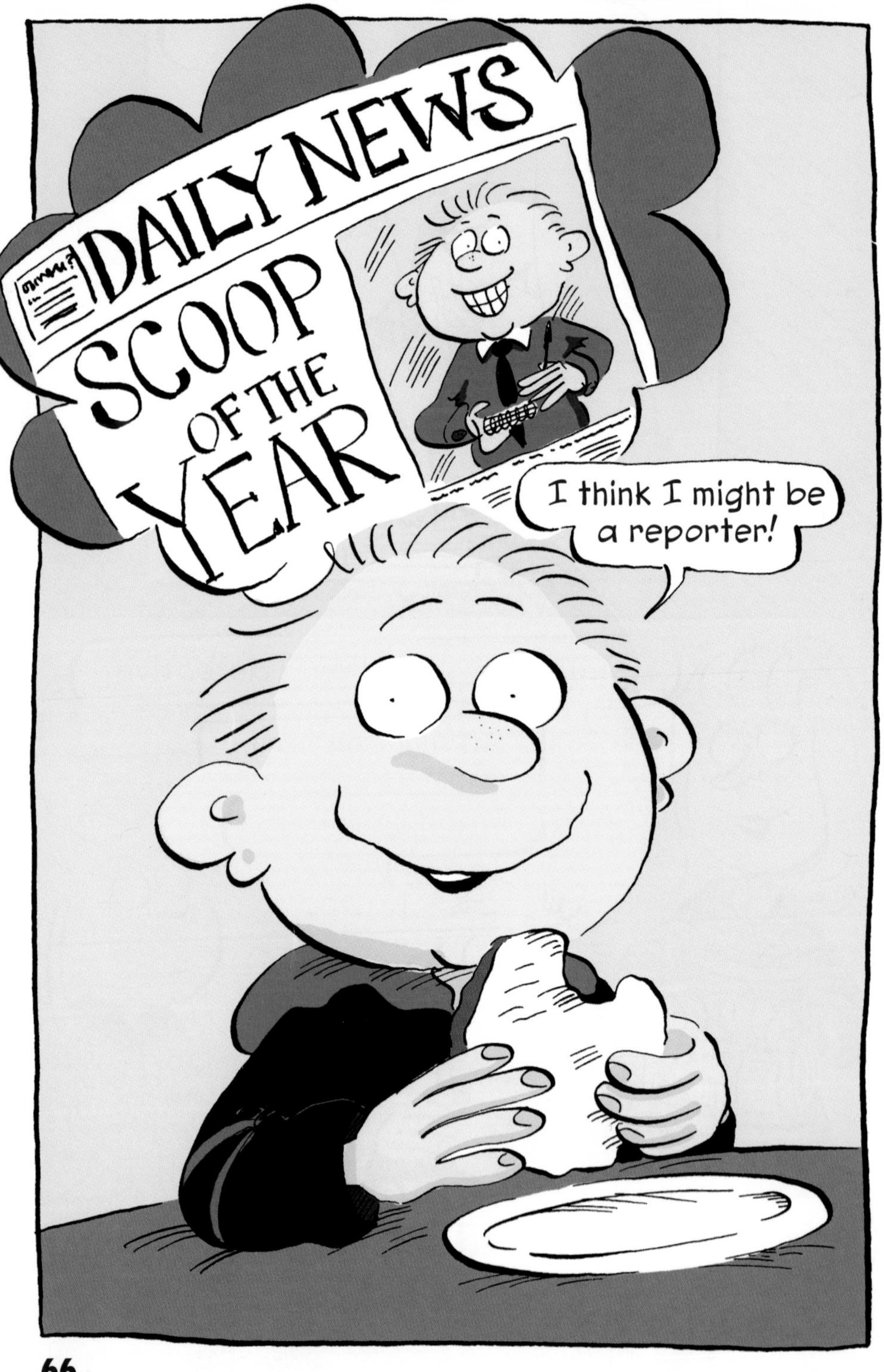
DAILY NEWS
SCOOP OF THE YEAR
I think I might be a reporter!

# ABOUT THE AUTHOR

Philip Wooderson has written more than twenty books for children, including the new young adult suspense novel, *The Plague, My Side of the Story.* Wooderson lives in England.

# ABOUT THE ILLUSTRATOR

Bridget MacKeith says that being an illustrator is the only thing she has ever wanted to be. Although she once thought of being an opera singer! MacKeith's artwork appears in dozens of children's books. She currently lives in a small town in the middle of the Salisbury Plain in England, with her husband, Gareth, her two children, and a big, hairy Newfoundland dog named Rudi. She also illustrates "a lot of cards for Hallmark."

# GLOSSARY

**cunning** (KUN-ing)—smart or clever

**detective** (di-TEK-tiv)—someone, usually a police officer, whose work is getting information about crimes and trying to solve them

**expedition** (ek-spuh-DISH-uhn)—a trip for exploring or studying something

**loot** (LOOT)—valuable things that have been stolen

**reporter** (ri-POR-tur)—someone who gathers and reports news, usually for a newspaper

**villain** (VIL-uhn)—someone who is wicked or evil

# INTERNET SITES

Do you want to know more about subjects related to this book? Or are you interested in learning about other topics? Then check out FactHound, a fun, easy way to find Internet sites.
Our investigative staff has already sniffed out great sites for you!
Here's how to use FactHound:

1. Visit *www.facthound.com*

2. Select your grade level.

3. To learn more about subjects related to this book, type in the book's ISBN number: **1598890859**.

4. Click the **Fetch It** button.

FactHound will fetch the best Internet sites for you.

# DISCUSSION QUESTIONS

1. What do you think about Arf opening his neighbor's mail? (It's actually against the law). How and why did he not get into trouble?

2. What do you know about metal detectors? How do they work? What would you do with one?

3. Why do you think Arf, at the end, says he'd rather be a reporter than a detective. Explain.

# WRITING PROMPTS

1. Arf was cheating when he had Bee bury the treasure for him. He would know right where it was before he and Gloria even reached the park. How you feel about cheating? Did someone ever cheat you? Write and tell what happened. Include how you felt about it.

2. Have you ever made a bet with someone, the way Arf and Gloria made their bet? Write about what happened.

3. If you had your own metal detector and found buried treasure with it, what would you do next? Write it out. Describe what kind of treasure you find, too.

# ALSO BY PHILIP WOODERSON

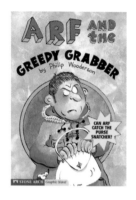

ARF AND THE
GREEDY GRABBER
by Philip Wooderson
CAN ARF CATCH THE PURSE SNATCHER?
STONE ARCH Graphic Novel

**Arf and the Greedy Grabber**

*Arf loves practical jokes. His tricks give him and his sisters a laugh . . . until a real thief turns up.*

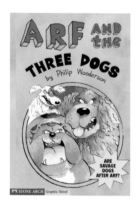

ARF AND THE
THREE DOGS
by Philip Wooderson
ARE SAVAGE DOGS AFTER ARF?
STONE ARCH Graphic Novel

**Arf and the Three Dogs**

*Someone is out to close down the dog pound! Will Arf find the evidence he needs to save it?*

**ORDER NOW!**

**STONE ARCH BOOKS,**
151 Good Counsel Hill Drive, Mankato, MN 56001
1-800-421-7731
www.stonearchbooks.com